BLOWING
in the WIND
A Novel

Joyce Webb Hahn

iUniverse

BLOWING IN THE WIND

iUniverse books may be ordered through booksellers or by contacting:

iUniverse
1663 Liberty Drive
Bloomington, IN 47403
www.iuniverse.com
1-800-Authors (1-800-288-4677)

Because of the dynamic nature of the Internet, any web addresses or links contained in this book may have changed since publication and may no longer be valid. The views expressed in this work are solely those of the author and do not necessarily reflect the views of the publisher, and the publisher hereby disclaims any responsibility for them.

Any people depicted in stock imagery provided by Thinkstock are models, and such images are being used for illustrative purposes only.
Certain stock imagery © Thinkstock.

ISBN: 978-1-4917-6364-3 (sc)
ISBN: 978-1-4917-6363-6 (e)

Print information available on the last page.

iUniverse rev. date: 4/6/2015

Acknowledgments

I wish to thank several people who helped me write this book: Peter and Susan Hahn, who lived through the 60's and 70's as students and who were able to inform me about the student lifestyle of that time; and members of my writers' group, Joan Condon, Natalya Dragunsky, Beverly Paik, Evelyn Smart and George Hahn.

Chapter One

S an Francisco State College, March,1969; Alone on the cement pathway, breathing rapidly, feeling vulnerable, Angela surveyed the deserted classroom buildings, the stretches of lawn, normally buzzing with students, but now empty, and with a shock to her spine, the remains of a bonfire still smoldering, scraps of partially burnt papers scattered around it, the steel gray of the sky pressing down upon its ashes. She felt as if she were lost in a war zone—in no-man's land. She moved quickly, continuing up the path, aware that the student and faculty demonstrators would be picketing in front of the administration building at the far end of the campus, which was where she was headed.

The silence was ominous and she clutched her portfolio tightly under her arm. Was it a mistake to come here? She'd crossed the bay from Berkeley hoping to finish collecting the signatures she needed to receive her Master's Degree, which meant going to the administration building. Due to the strike, which she'd supported, she hadn't been on campus for four months. She stared ahead, her eyes and ears sharply alert. It was so quiet. Eerily so. She began to climb the cement steps going up the slope that led to California Hall, the education building. She paused on the steps. Should she go home, return later when the strike was over? No. She needed the transcripts for her job.

She moved on, remaining alert, darting glances from side to side, unsure of what to expect. At the top of the steps she suddenly stopped, anchored to the spot, her throat constricted. Ahead, in the shadow of the building, a column of tall uniformed police stood in formation, four men across, the black visors on their helmets pulled down over their faces, shields held steady, night sticks and gun holsters hanging from their black leather belts. They stood like sinister statues, stealthy, unmoving, not uttering a sound. It was the Tactical Squad, she realized, hiding, waiting in silence for their orders to attack.

Then she heard the gunshot. She didn't hesitate, but pivoted on the spot and raced down the hill to her car, her heart pounding. She didn't belong here. She had a family to care for. Within seconds she'd started her car and raced out onto Nineteenth Ave heading for the bridge to Berkeley.

As she drove through the city traffic she turned on her car radio, hoping to find a news station. At the first stoplight she twisted the dial until she heard the excited voice of a newscaster speaking over the clamor of yelling, shouting people she assumed were striking students. *It's the riot police, the tactical squad in black helmets and shields. They're dragging the strikers down the stairs, their placards trampled on the administration building steps, their black power demands ignored.* Angela took a deep breath, and when the station switched to a commercial she turned off the radio. She clutched the steering wheel with shaking hands as she drove rapidly through the traffic. She still felt like running, racing away from the confrontation.

When she reached the bay bridge she reduced her speed and forced herself to consider what she'd just witnessed. And what about the gunshot she'd heard? Had there been more weapons in protesters' hands? Panthers had been told to carry guns for self protection, they called it, which scared her. She'd heard their rhetoric, their rage at whites. She was white and therefore their enemy, even if she told them she'd been a staunch advocate of civil rights or that her great grandparents in Maine had harbored escaped slaves for the Underground Railway. So far nobody on campus had been shot, thank God, but there was the gunshot she heard. Had anyone been hit?

She then thought about her younger son, Kim, a student at U.C. Berkeley. She knew he was involved in anti-war activities on campus. Would Kim be confronted by riot police and risk being expelled from the university? He was nineteen, almost twenty, and was registered for the draft, claiming a student deferral. The thought of either of her sons being drafted and sent to fight in Vietnam was just too terrible to contemplate. Kim had at least two more years as an undergraduate, but Michael would graduate from Stanford soon, ending his student deferral to the draft. Some of her sons' friends threatened to defy the draft board and escape to Canada. It seemed as if students everywhere were going crazy these days—even in France and England—and they weren't threatened by the Vietnam War.

It was certainly damned difficult to be a parent these days. What with drugs like LSD, idiots like Timothy Leary exhorting your kids to turn on and drop out—and the guns toted by the Panthers in Oakland and the Venceremos in Palo Alto, and now at her own college, where she'd heard a gunshot. It was too much, overwhelming. And not only students were in a frenzy. Last year the assassinations of Martin Luther King and Robert Kennedy shocked the entire nation. And Kennedy was shot while being filmed on TV!

By now she'd crossed the bridge and turned off onto University Avenue. She and Hank lived on Keith street, north of the campus on the hill overlooking the bay in a large redwood-shingled house. Kim stayed in the guest house in the back of the property, choosing to save money and forgo campus dorm life.

When she entered their driveway, she was surprised to see his VW Bug with the porcupine painted on it's hood parked at the side of the house. Why was he still home? She glanced at her watch. Ten o'clock. Normally he had classes at this time. Could U.C. be on strike again? This was Kim's sophomore year and he was working toward a degree in Architecture, which included math and engineering, which he couldn't afford to cut—or miss. Failure was not an option with the threat of the draft hanging over his head like a guillotine.

As she walked up the path to the house the sight of the pink blossoms on the flowering plum tree cheered her a little. And the fog had lifted, revealing a brilliant blue sky. She took a deep breath. She was beginning to relax a little. And she really needed to stop worrying about her sons. They were no longer children, after all. Just as she was mounting the steps to the house, she heard the joyful bark of the family border collie, Angus, who was galloping around the side of the house to greet her, his tongue lolling from his mouth in a happy smile. "Hello, Angus, good boy. I'm happy to see you, too." And she was. Angus' energy and enthusiasm helped raise her spirits. She glanced again at the blossoming tree before unlocking the door. Angus bounded into the house ahead of her.

The first thing she did after closing the front door was to pick up the phone on the hall table and dial Hank's lab. He knew she was going to San Francisco to have her papers signed and would be worried about her if he'd heard about the police action at SF State. He picked up on the first ring. "Angela," he said, sounding relieved, "where are you?"

"I just got home, and I'm fine." She recounted what she had seen and heard at SF State, but reassured him she was OK, that she had left as soon as she had heard the gunshot. "I'll have to wait until the strike is over before I go back again. My Master's can wait."

"Good. I'm relieved. Scott told me he'd heard about the turmoil there on the radio on his way to work. So, any other news since I saw you this morning?"

"Not really. Kim seems to be here, but I haven't seen him. At least his car is here."

"He probably overslept. Stop worrying. OK? Well, I've got to go. See you tonight. I'm glad you called. So long, doll."

"Bye." She hung up the phone, tugged off her jacket and tossed it on a chair. She'd think about Kim later. Now she needed to relax. She collapsed on the living room couch and picked up her sketch book she'd left on the coffee table. She idly turned the pages, glancing briefly at her drawings, trying to stop thinking about the scene at State, but the image of the black-garbed Tac Squad hiding in the shadow of the education building kept jamming her brain.

About an hour later, she heard Kim's voice calling from the back door. "Mom, are you home?" He ran into the room, breathing hard. "I just now heard on the radio about the trouble at SF State this

4

morning. Those riot police can be vicious, and I remembered you were going there today. Are you OK?"

"Yeah, I'm fine, I guess."

"So what happened? Were you in that mess? You look kind of wiped out."

"I left as soon as I saw the Tac Squad waiting in the wings, with their shields and nightsticks. And when I heard the gunshot I rushed back to my car I'll need to go again when the strike is over, if it ever is."

Kim grinned. "Not many other guys I know have mothers who've fled from the riot police. "I'm glad you're OK, Mom." He sat down beside her and clapped her on the shoulder. She tried to smile.

"I think I'd like some coffee," she said, moving toward the kitchen. "Join me?"

"Sure, why not," and he followed her into the kitchen.

She peered at Kim as she poured water into the kettle, still wondering why he was home, but reluctant to broach the subject. It would be good to have a chat free from her prying and his defensiveness. She managed a wry smile. They could share experiences about student demonstrations. She watched him as he sprawled on the kitchen chair, Angus lying at his feet at his usual place under the table. Kim had grown so tall these last few years, and he was so very handsome with his wide gray eyes and high cheekbones. His face had developed sharper angles and now that his curly, russet-colored hair was clustered around his ears he was quite striking. There must be girls, of course. He would attract them. He didn't admit to a serious girlfriend, but she knew he had a following. She'd heard their voices on the phone.

"So, Mom, tell me what you saw? The police were pretty rough on the protesters, the radio reporter said. Did you see any of that?"

She shook her head, spooning Peet's coffee into the Melitta filter. "No. When I saw those policemen in all their black gear and heard the gunshot I ran like hell." The kettle shrieked and she poured the water into the filter top. "Those police were scary. Their black uniforms and shiny plastic shields and visors make them look like monsters in a horror film."

"So do you think there's a chance that the trustees will ever agree to the strikers' demands? I hear the Black Students Union has teamed up with the Third World Liberation Front."

"Who knows? I've lost track of all their demands. The main one is to create a Black Studies program and to reinstate George Murray."

"He's the Black Panther guy, right?"

"Right. Their Minister of Education, whatever that means. He made a well-publicized speech at Fresno State saying that blacks were slaves and the only way to become free was to kill their slave masters. Then at SF State he said that students should bring guns to campus to protect themselves from racist white administrators. Obviously the Trustees were outraged and forced his suspension."

"And the strike began."

"And has gone on for four months now." She poured the filtered coffee into the two mugs, handed him one and sat opposite him at the table. "But, Kim, enough of SF State. What's happening here at Berkeley. I know the strike the Third World Liberation Front called is over, thank God, but what's all this about a park? You're involved somehow, right?

Kim set down his coffee, his face lighting up. "There's a bunch of us who want to make a park out of that mess that has been made on that university property south side of campus over by Dwight Way and Haste St. I'm writing a piece about it for the Daily Cal. That's why I stayed home this morning. I guess I was concentrating so hard I didn't hear your car drive up."

"I read something about that property a while ago. The university planned to make a parking lot and a sports field. Then they ran out of money?"

"Right. They condemned and took over the old houses and buildings, demolished them, but before they could fix it up the funds dried up. Everyone knows they just wanted to get rid of all the hippies living in the cheap housing south of campus, but now the space is full of debris, wrecked cars, and garbage." Kim paused to take a sip of coffee. "Some of us think we should turn the land into a public park. The hippies want to plant things, have an attractive place for concerts—all that—and the political groups want a place to meet, to organize, to have our anti-war rallies. We need a place that isn't controlled like Sproul Plaza."

Angela poured more coffee. "And the administration's reaction?"

"We're not sure. We think if we just go ahead and start the work, get rid of the junk, plant things, they'll be pleased about it." He laughed. "Maybe. Unless they think it's a plot cooked up by the Free Speech Movement or other radical groups."

Angela gave him an appraising glance. "Well, you're involved in FSM aren't you?"

"Yeah, lots of us are. We believe in our Constitutional rights. What's wrong with that?" His voice took on a defensive tone.

Angela shrugged, then grinned. "Not a thing." She rose and picked up the empty mugs and set them in the sink, deciding not to continue the conversation. She'd been treading on thin ice. Kim had left the table and had headed for the back door, Angus following. Kim glanced over his shoulder and grinned. "Anyway, I'm glad you got home safe. We live in exciting times. Right?" and he closed the door behind him.

Chapter Two

Stanford, April, 1969; The door to the computer room swung closed behind him, shutting away the the humming of electronic connections and whirling discs. His shift at the computer lab over, Michael opened the heavy main door, stepped out onto the stone building's corridor and took a deep breath of the mild, fresh air. He could smell the fragrance of spring flowers, and when he peered upward he noted the stars emerging in the darkening sky. As he strode down the steps, he spied two students walking along the corridor carrying Stop Classified Research placards. He swore under his breath, fucking idiots, and headed for the bicycle rack.

It was a fine evening and he wanted to forget about the political turmoil here on the campus, which was impossible, of course. He was surrounded by anti-war activists—even at the house he shared with three other students. His eyes lingered on the pair with the placards, and wondered what had happened at the big rally that afternoon. All the peace organizations had been invited to attend, and If it hadn't been for his job he might have gone just to know what was going on. The anti-war people were demanding that Stanford ban government-funded classified research. And if they didn't get research money from the governent, where would it come from? And what would that mean for Michael's grad program in Applied Physics?

He unlocked his bike from the rack and as he pedaled by the student union, he considered stopping for something to eat and to hear news about the rally, but decided against it. He still had work to do on a problem set for his Communications Theory class, so he'd just rustle up something at home. It only took him fifteen minutes to pedal to the clapboard house the four of them rented north of the campus just off Stanford Ave. He found two of his housemates, Alistair, a Poly Sci major, and Julie, an English major, sitting at the kitchen table, a large pizza, between them. The third housemate, Ron, was probably at a rehearsal. Ron was a theater arts major.

Alistair whose wavy blond hair hung to his shoulders, hailed him as he entered. "Hey, man, you're just in time. Julie's treat."

Michael tugged off his faded blue corduroy jacket and shot Julie an astonished look. Pizza wasn't exactly her style. "Have you decided pizza's OK now, Julie?"

She laughed, her blue eyes shining. "No, Michael. I liberated it after the rally. This pizza was left on a table outside Dinkelspiel. It may be junk food, but we're hungry."

Michael pulled up a chair and reached for a triangle of pizza from the box Julie had shoved toward him. "So how did the rally go? Did you come to any conclusions? And I'm surprised you SDS guys are still at it. I thought Sudents for a Democratic Society was disintegrating. Or going militant."

Julie picked up a napkin and mopped pizza sauce from her hands and mouth. Her voice sparked with excitement. "Not us. We're non-violent. And the rally went great. Hundreds of students came. And some faculty, too. And we voted to demand the university to stop doing the fucking classified research, that it isn't the role of a great university. The trustees will be meeting in five days and a committee will present the demands. If they disagree we'll demonstrate. Take over."

Alistair pushed back his chair, moved to the refrigerator and brought out some bottles of Budweiser. He handed one to Michael, who quickly opened it and took a long swallow, wondering what department the students would be attacking. Alistair remained standing, gripping the back of his chair, his tall form poised as if for action. "And we're especially against the Stanford Research Institute. They've done stuff for CIA. Chemical weapons, communication systems for fighter planes—and our pilots drop napalm bombs on Vietnamese children from those planes." He shot Michael a stern look with his dark blue eyes, blue like the sea at Penobscot Bay in Maine, Michael thought wryly, where Alistair kept his sailboat. "And our demands are fucking non-negotiable."

"Right on, Alistair! Fucking non-negotiable!" Julie cried.

Micheal regarded his housemates with a wary look. "And which department will be your target?"

Alistair gave him a defiant stare "We're considering the Applied Electronics Lab."

"Shit, Alistair. They fund my computer lab. My job. Christ, this school needs government money for research. Where else would we get it?"

"It's just the classified stuff we want to stop."

Julie chimed in, tossing a long strand of blonde hair back over her shoulder. "Michael, you know what we're doing to the Vietnamese people! It's got to be stopped!"

Alistair straddled his chair and nailed Michael with a hard look. "And have you read about the draft lottery congress is talking about? We'll be getting numbers. They'll put our fucking birth dates on pieces of paper and toss them into a bowl and then fish them out. One by one."

"But we'll still get our student deferrals, right?"

"They say we will, but shit, you never know. People are bitching. They say the army is made up of the poor and lower-middle class. College types like us are opting out. They think it's unfair."

Julie peered up at Alistair, her face aglow. "But if our protests work, the war would end and you wouldn't get drafted!"

Michael threw Julie an exasperated look. "Julie, you're crazy if you think your sit-ins and marches will stop the war. Nothing will stop the war until people realize the Vietnamese won't let us win! But God knows if that will ever happen."

He shoved back his chair, swallowed the last of his beer, thanked Julie for the pizza and headed for the stairs to one of the two rooms in the attic to work on his problem set. Ron's room was opposite his. Julie and Alistair's rooms were downstairs.

Although his room was small, it had a window that looked out over neighboring roof tops and the greening hills beyond. His desk was under the window and books were jammed into the bookcase next to it. Papers were stacked tidily on the desk. On the floor under the eaves was a mattress covered by an army blanket and an assortment of pillows.

As Michael turned on the desk lamp and closed the faded blue cotton curtains over the window, he found himself replaying the conversation he'd just heard. He felt a mounting impatience with Julie's naïveté, of Alistair's self-satisfied, rich-boy's certainty, his belief in the rightness of his cause. What did anybody really know about Vietnam? As far as he, Michael, was concerned, the war was a mistake, unnecessary. The Vietnamese fought for their independence from France, and if America had supported their cause instead of aiding our ally, France, we wouldn't be embroiled in this mess. But the anti-war protests hadn't brought peace. Wouldn't it be wiser to hone your skills and try to make a difference from within the establishment?

Michael thought about his Dad's tales about meeting Ho Chi Minh in 1945 when as an American soldier, an interpreter, he'd been parachuted into the Viet Nimh guerrilla camp by the OSS. He'd been on a team assigned to help the guerillas fight the Japanese occupiers. He'd admired Ho and said Ho was pro-American, pro-democracy, although a Communist, of course. Dad had also told him the information was sensitive, that he'd been questioned by the FBI about his experience with Ho and General Giap, and had been concerned about keeping his all-important security clearance.

He was a physicist working at the Livermore Rad Lab and kept his ambivalent feelings about the war to himself. His former boss had been Edward Teller, known for being in charge of the development of the hydrogen bomb, a top secret project, of course. People here at Stanford who did classified work for the government needed security clearances, too—as did some of the students. His own job at the computer lab was not classified, thank God. His SDS housemates would not be an asset!

Michael sighed, shuffled the stack of papers on his desk and tugged out the problem set assignment he needed for his communications theory class. He forced himself to set aside his concerns about the war, the draft, the protesters. He had work to do.

On a Monday evening four days later, when Michael walked into the kitchen to make himself some coffee, he found all three of his housemates excitedly grabbing their belongings, pulling on jackets, ready to leave. He'd heard that the trustees had refused to consider the SDS demands and that the peace groups had voted to demonstrate. Unfortunately, SDS members chose the Applied Electronics Lab for the sit-in. As he filled the kettle with water and set in on the stove, Julie moved to the door. "We've got to go, you guys. This is it." She picked up her Ibiza basket from the floor beside her chair and slung the handles over her shoulder. Michael noted she was wearing her best Salvation Army- purchased black jacket over her jeans. A red peasant kerchief tied back her long blonde hair. She looked up at Michael and tossed him a radiant smile. "I guess we're ready. So, we'll see you later, Michael. You're not joining us, obviously, but maybe you'll drop by? We agreed that people could come in or out of the lab at any time. We'll just be sitting there. Peacefully."

Ron, whose curly dark hair was expertly combed up into an afro and whose jeans displayed a tanned knee through a frayed hole, picked up a notebook and what looked like a play script. "We'll keep up our work while we stay there."

"What about food?" Michael asked. "You might be there for a while. You know how long it takes for academics to make decisions."

Alistair adjusted the red scarf tied over his forehead and took a last sip of coffee. "People promised to bring us stuff."

Ron laughed, raising his eyebrows. "Like maybe a little help from our friends?"

Alistair frowned. "But nothing illegal, Ron. We can't give Prisker any excuse to call in the pigs. And no violence. Think of Ghandi."

Chapter Three

Berkeley, April, 1969; As Kim opened the door of his black VW bug, he eyed the hippie-style porcupine he'd painted on its hood. He really must paint it over one of these days. He'd outgrown that hippie shit. He backed the car out of the driveway and headed for campus. The morning fog had lifted, and as he drove down the hill he could catch glimpses of the San Francisco skyline beyond the stretch of the bay. On the seat beside him was a copy of the *Berkeley Barb*. He'd picked it up yesterday and had been impressed by Stew Albert's piece about clearing the unused university land to make a people's park. Surely, the article would cause a stir. His own letter to the Daily Cal had attracted attention, but counter-culture *Barb* had a wider audience. Albert had done a good job describing the meeting the local residents had called last week. They wanted the mess cleaned up, he'd written, and agreed a park would be great. It wouldn't only be for anti-war rallies or student strike meetings, but a place for anyone to enjoy.

By now Kim had arrived at the campus parking lot. He found a spot, picked up his notebook and the newspaper from the seat, locked his car and headed for the library. It was Sunday and he didn't have classes, but he needed to work on a research paper for his Architecture Design class. He had the afternoon free and intended to walk over to the proposed park property with Gina Olivetti. She'd agreed to meet him at Sproul Plaza at noon.

The thought of seeing Gina brightened the day. He'd met her at a poster-making session for Free Speech Movement a month ago, and they'd hit it off right away. She was political, of course, anti-Vietnam

13

war, like everyone else he knew, and she was also beautiful and smart. He'd never felt such a strong attraction for a girl as he did with Gina. He wanted to be with her all the time. It had taken him a while before he had the courage to ask her out. He'd noted the other guys who hung around her, but she'd said yes to his invitation to go to a movie with him and they'd been seeing each other almost every day since then.

A little before noon, after he left the library, he hurried to Sproul Hall steps were he'd agreed to meet Gina. The plaza was buzzing with students standing in clumps or striding off to favorite haunts on Telegraph or Bancroft Avenues or gathered around tables set up by a variety of organizations, several of them political. Kim was pleased to see how many anti-Vietnam war posters were displayed. They could thank Mario Savio for that. Four years ago Mario had won the right for students to champion political causes next to these steps. Now, opposite the steps Kim spied the Free Speech Movement table manned by a student he didn't know who was deep in conversation with Ron Delaine, one of the older radical leaders, no longer a student.

Then from the direction of Sather Gate he caught a glimpse of Gina, maneuvering through a clutch of students, her light brown, waist-long hair shining in the sunlight. She wore a loose green blouse over her jeans and he watched with pleasure how she seemed to float as she moved through Sather Gate. He waved to her and shouldered his way through the crowd to reach her, trying to catch her glance. He loved how the color of her eyes could change from blue or green with specks of gold as the light shifted. Now they were a soft green-gold and filled with light. "Hi, Gina," he called, waving again. Their glances connected and she threw him a warm smile. When he reached her side he touched her arm lightly, murmured a soft greeting, and they moved as one toward Telegraph Avenue.

Gina gestured to the students around them. "Do you think people will have read the Barb? Will they be coming with us?"

He scanned the crowd. "We'll soon find out. We'll be there in ten minutes or so"

As they passed the FSM table, they exchanged greetings with Delaine who turned to join them. Kim noted his shoulder-length blond hair and the loose crinkly Indian shirt that glittered with tiny mirrors. "I assume you're headed to the park site," Delaine said, pulling a pair of work gloves from the back pocket of his jeans. "Lot's of junk on that lot."

"Yeah," Kim answered. "I wonder if anyone will come to help."

Gina eyed the work gloves. "Let's hope so."

Ron shot Gina a sharp glance. "They'll be there, I'm sure. The Barb piece will bring them in. All the anti-war groups, leftists, counter culture people, hippies. . .it will create an issue, unify, bring different types of people together."

Gina laughed, fingering the blue beads hanging around her slender neck. "Some of my friends just want a pleasant place to have concerts and smoke. Or plant flowers and dance."

Kim nodded. "But the anti-war people want a place to organize, to have rallies, demonstrations." He glanced at the students who streamed along the avenue. Some had ambled into coffee shops, book stores or to idle by the sidewalk artisans selling their wares, but there was still those who strode forward.

By now they'd turned the corner at Haste street. Delaine was tugging on his gloves. "Well, one thing for sure, when our dear Governor hears of it, he'll be sucked in. We'll have an issue, all right, and we'll give him a fight. I've been waiting for this." He clenched a fist as he spoke.

Kim thought of the vows Reagan had made during his election campaign for governor. He remembered Reagan's infuriating words. He'd promised to crack down on university administrators for permitting the Berkeley campus to become a haven for "communist sympathizers, protesters and sex deviants." Kim hadn't been able to forget that phrase. And Californians had elected the bastard, and it was the governor who appointed the all-powerful board of trustees.

When they drew close to the site of the proposed park they spied a crowd of busy workers ahead. Kim stopped and stared. "Jesus, look! There must be a hundred people here already."

Ron clapped his gloved hands and let out a gleeful "far out! Albert's piece in the Barb brought them in! We're going to have ourselves a fucking park!"

Kim and Gina, both laughing and whooping, rushed forward to join the horde. People with shovels were turning the soil. Others were carrying young trees and shrubs set in nursery cans, and two pickup trucks were already piled with refuse. A man Kim recognized as a well-known Berkeley landscape architect was shouting out directions to students turning the soil. Two pretty students in loose Guatemalan Mayan blouses worn over cut-off jeans were placing loaves of brown bread and jars of homemade jams on a camping table someone had set up. Kim grabbed a shovel and Gina picked up a small pine tree and they joined the crew.

While Kim was toiling at the park site, his parents were sunning themselves on their deck that looked out over the San Francisco bay. They sat in two identical redwood chairs, and on the redwood table next to Hank was an untidy scattering of newspapers. His head, with its receding hairline, leaned back against the chair. His light brown eyes were focused on the view, and he held a cigarette between his fingers. Angela, who sat next to him, was sipping coffee from a brown earthenware mug. Lazily, Hank picked up the front page of the San Francisco Chronicle and scanned the headlines. Lowering the paper, he glanced at Angela. "Now that the strike at State is over will you try again to get the signatures you need?"

She shrugged. "I'll wait a while. It was just so chaotic on that campus. And who knows if the agreement will really stick."

Hank suddenly thought of seeing SF State President Hayakawa on TV, in a rage, pulling out the wires of the sound system during a student protest. He gave a rueful smile and tapped at the page. "It's amazing the Committee actually agreed to all those demands, and from both the Black Power and the Third World Liberation people." Hank sighed. "I wish there was a way to stop the demonstrators from picketing the Livermore lab. There's no way the government is going to give in to their demands."

16

Angela set her coffee mug onto the redwood table. "I wish there was a way to stop the demonstrations everywhere. Both Cal and State campuses are in turmoil. I wonder what's happening at Stanford right now. The SDS students have called a sit-in at the Applied Electronics Lab, apparently." She pointed to the newspaper Hank held in his hands. It's on the second page."

Hank quickly turned the page and scanned the article. "Yeah, they've taken over, it says, but they're not stopping anyone from entering." He gave an abrupt laugh. "There won't be much work going on with all those students crowding the corridors and labs." He thought of Michael who might have classes in that building. "I hope Michael isn't doing work there."

Angela fixed her eyes on the hills across the bay. "I hope he isn't taking part in the sit-in."

Hank gave her a sharp look. "He better not be. It's bad enough that Kim is so involved with this park business. There's my security clearance to worry about."

"At least Kim hasn't picketed your lab—like some of his friends with their ban the bomb and get out of Vietnam placards."

Hank tossed the paper onto the table and stubbed out his cigarette in a glass ashtray. "Yeah." He leaned back in the chair and peered up at the blue sky. The photograph of the mushroom cloud over the Bikini Atoll test site flashed into his mind—and the pictures of the fishermen who had been victims of test fallout. When he thought of the bomb a sick feeling slid into his gut. Lately, he'd been finding himself in sympathy with the protestors. How did he get sucked into this work? Herbert York had persuaded him, of course, assuring him that he'd have a strong physics section, but the Pentagon funded nuclear weapons research and that's what he'd been stuck with the last few years. Maybe this new bio-medical division will be more palatable. He'd often considered moving to another job, to some physics department in a small university that wasn't engaged in defense work, but he loved Berkeley, and there was Angela's teaching job and the boys' schools, so they'd stayed here in a kind of inertia.

He shifted in his chair and gazed at Angela, who had picked up the newspaper. She was a lovely woman, although her clear gray eyes looked troubled. And why shouldn't she be troubled. The country was in turmoil. The Vietnam war was tearing the country apart, and at the moment Berkeley seemed to be in the center of it. And Kim was in its midst, taking an active role in its protests, speaking out against the war. Not only did Kim risk his expulsion from university and being sent to Vietnam, but his reputation as a radical, a leftist, could bring on doubts about his own loyalty to the government, his top secret security clearance. In the current political climate, tenured positions for physicists would be non-existent without one, even at small universities, and anyway, he'd become intrigued by the new bio-medical project at the lab. He needed his security clearance.

He remembered the FBI interviews he'd had to go through in the 50's. His file would still contain the information about his contact with Ho Chi Minh during World War II. He'd been cleared then, but would Kim's actions cause the NSA to have another, closer, look at his case? During the 50's interrogation we were at war with Korea. Now we were at war in Vietnam against the Vietcong, and Ho Chi Min was its hero.

He was startled from his reflections by the sound of the telephone ringing from inside the house. Angela hopped up and moved quickly into the living room. He could hear her voice, a voice that was so expressive and musical. It was Michael. Good, he thought, Michael could tell them what was happening at Stanford and how he was coping with the mess. He just hoped the boy stayed out of it. So far Michael had been keeping out of campus protests and was a serious student. He wasn't sure, but Michael might be doing some of his work at the Electronics lab. If the students were crowding the labs it would have to be difficult, if not impossible to concentrate, to think. He would be graduating in June if all went well and hopefully would be going to grad school next fall. If not, the draft board would be after him. At that thought, Hank rose and strode into the house. He needed to talk to the boy.

Chapter Four

May, 1969, Stanford; It was after midnight when Michael left the computer room. He'd fed the IBM cards with his program and data into the card reader and now must wait a few hours for the computer to crunch the numbers. As he trudged to the bike rack outside the building, he glanced into the darkness toward the Applied Electronics Lab. It seemed quiet tonight. The demonstrators had finally voted to end their sit-in, thank God, but he could hear a rumble of voices from Hoover Tower. Wouldn't they ever go home? He groaned. He was so tired, so very, very tired of it all. He pushed back the unruly strands of thick brown hair that fell over his brow and mounted his bike.

As he pedaled across campus the chaotic events of the past week kept whirling through his head. The sit-in at AEL had gone on for a miserable nine days. It had been impossible to do any work at the lab for his advanced computer course and when he attempted to work at home, all three of his housemates were in an out of the house at odd hours clumping about, talking loudly. They'd all been in the midst of the protest. Julie never seemed to stop screaming about the wickedness of weapons research, how it was responsible for the napalm bombings and burned babies in Vietnam. A huge rally of students had called for a one-day strike and students and faculty both had demanded the end of classified research on the campus. Then much to his dismay the head of AEL had declared he would no longer accept security contracts, which would mean the loss of government funding for the lab.

During all the uproar he'd been working night and day trying to finish his projects. The end of the semester was approaching along with finals and his graduation. It was imperative he finish his assignments and do well on his finals. He'd been accepted as a grad student in Applied Physics here at Stanford, but it depended on his completing his undergraduate courses—which had been damned near impossible to do these last few weeks. Furthermore he knew that much of the graduate research work in the Physics department was classified and funded by the government. Would losing research funding force the department to reduce the size of it's graduate program? If he suddenly found himself turned down here at Stanford it would be impossible to be immediately accepted at some other university. The draft board would be waiting for him. If he didn't have the fucking student deferral he could end up in Vietnam.

The noise from the other side of Hoover Tower grew louder and as his long legs pedaled closer he realized that a crowd had gathered in front of Encina Hall, the administration building. What now? One of the students had mounted the steps and with waving arms was shouting in loud exclamatory tones. Yelling students trotted toward the building from all directions, impeding Michael's progress. He dismounted from his bike and with his hands on the handlebars tried to push his way through the horde of oncoming students. One of the figures that swarmed around his bike turned out to be Julie, his blonde housemate. "Hey, Michael, you're going the wrong way," Julie called out, moving toward him.

"I'm going home, Julie. To sleep," Michael yelled, inching forward.

Julie maneuvered closer. "Come on, Michael! We're taking over Encina Hall. We can't give up the fight. It's too fucking important. Think of all those burned babies!"

Michael gave a dismissive shake of his head and continued wheeling his bike through the crowd. "See you later, Julie," and fuck you, he mumbled under his breath. He was sick to death of Julie's dramatic catch phrases. He finally escaped the throng, remounted his bike and pedaled home. Wearily, he climbed the stairs to his room, set his alarm for 5 o'clock, and removing only his shoes flopped into bed. When his clock's piercing ring forced him awake, he tried to ignore it, clamping his eyes tightly shut. The ringing persisted, and cursing, he reached to shut if off. In the bathroom he threw water on his face, squinting in the light that shone down on him from over the mirror, noting his bloodshot brown eyes and stubbly chin. He felt like hell, but he needed to get to the computer room to pick up his results. Had his program worked? If not he'd need to try again today.

After quickly fixing himself some coffee he mounted his bike once more and headed for campus. The sky was lightening. When he pedaled along Campus Drive he was shocked to see he was being overtaken by a rapidly-moving parade of police cars and vans jammed with police officers, their headlights still shining. He dismounted, pushed his bike onto the walk beside the street and stared. As they sped by he could see that the vehicles were marked as belonging to the County Sheriff's Department. At the corner they turned up Serra street. Cautiously, Michael followed.

From a spot that he considered safe, he watched as the armed police poured from their halted vehicles and sprinted toward the administration building. The men approached in columns. At the entrance to the lighted building they peeled off, forming a line surrounding the premises. Another column of men burst through the doors of the building, their hands on the batons at their sides. Next to one of the vans an officer shouted into a microphone, a speaker blaring from the roof of the van. "This is the Sheriff of Santa Clara county speaking. We have been called by President Pitzer to clear the building. Demonstrators must leave the premises immediately. Proceed at once. Peacefully, speedily. Disperse to your domiciles. Go home."

Michael held his breath. Would the students leave peacefully? Would they stick to their non-violent pledge? And would they be arrested? The sky was turning gray and a pink glow lit the eastern horizon. He could see the action clearly. As he watched, and as the police continued to enter the building, a trickle of silent students moved slowly out the doors and down the steps. Some had blankets draped around their shoulders. Most focused their eyes straight ahead, avoiding the stern glances of the police. Soon, the trickle became a surge, and all the demonstrators left the building. And to Michael's surprise and relief they wandered away, presumably to their dorms or residences. Not one of them was arrested. It wasn't long before the police poured our of the building and began to depart.

Michael took in a deep breath. He glanced at his watch. Seven o'clock. The building had been cleared in less than an hour. So that was that. What would happen next? He mounted his bike and headed for the computer room knowing he had to stick to his own tasks and get on with it.

Chapter Five

May 1969, Berkeley: The phone was ringing. The sound had incorporated itself into Kim's dream and the ringing continued until he decided he was awake. As he reached for the phone he glanced at his alarm clock and grunted. Who would call him at quarter to six in the morning? He finally managed to bring the receiver to his ear. It was Gina. Her voice was sharp with alarm. "Kim, wake up. Now! I just got a call from my friend Ann about the park. She lives on Haste Street. She says the park's swarming with police. Huge numbers. They're fencing it off—clearing a big area and pulling up our plants and trees. We've got to do something!"

"Shit! What the hell? Heyns promised he'd warn us if they were going to start working on the sports field. What's happening?"

"Ann doesn't know much. She just saw the police when she heard the commotion and looked outside her window. She went out to see if she could find out what they were doing, but they yelled at her to get out of there, that they were clearing the area—at Governor Reagan's orders, they said. She tried to get hold of some of guys on the committee and it was news to them, but they were going to check it out."

Kim had disentangled himself from the sheets and was on his feet as he listened to Gina's tale. The dog, Angus, who slept in Kim's room, had come toward him, for a morning greeting. "Gina," Kim said quickly, "where are you now?"

"In my room." Gina lived in a co-op residence just off Bancroft.

"Gina, can you meet me at Sather Gate? Let's see what we can find out, OK?' Gina agreed and Kim hung up the phone and grabbed the clothes he'd dropped on the floor the night before. After using the bathroom he picked up his car keys, opened the door for Angus, and raced to his car. "Stay, Angus!" he called out, then backed out the driveway.

Gina was waiting for him at Sather Gate. She stood alone. It was only six thirty in the morning, a Thursday. Classes didn't start until eight and only a handful of students walked the paths and streets. Gina rushed forward, calling his name. She wore a sweater the color of lemons over her jeans, and her long hair was tied back with a yellow scarf. Her eyes sparked with anger. "I can't believe those idiots would destroy our plants. My trees were taking root!"

Kim grabbed her hand and they rushed down Telegraph Ave toward the park. Just before they reached it, near the corner of Haste and Bowditch, they were stopped by a blockade of police cars and vans. Beyond the blockade Kim was stunned by the sight of the California Highway Police guarding a newly erected eight-foot high chain link fence stretching down both streets. From inside the fenced area he could see police tossing piles of destroyed plants and small trees into a dump truck. "Jesus," he said under his breath. "I can't believe it! Those fucking bastards!" He glanced at Gina and stretched his arm around her shoulders. Tears welled in her eyes and fell over paper-white cheeks.

As they stood there, staring, a Berkeley police car stopped beside them. The cop yelled, "get out of here! The area is closed until further notice! Go! Now!"

Before Kim could ask who had ordered the closure, the cop had turned the corner onto Bowditch continuing a slow prowl along the fence. As Kim and Gina continued to stare at the blockade of police and the tall fence, they were joined by a scattering of onlookers, eyes wide with shock—then rage.

Gina turned to Kim, and fishing a Kleenex from her jeans' pocket, blew her nose. "Let's spread the word. We've got to stop them."

And the word did spread. Free Speech Movement members went into action and at noon in Sproul Plaza, where a rally had been called to discuss the Israeli-Palestinian conflict, the FSM and others who'd worked to create the park crammed the plaza, yelling to be heard. Kim and Gina were in their midst. Gina was eying the campus police patrolling the plaza's perimeter.

Kim watched as Michael Lerner, the student activist scheduled to lead the discussion, turned the meeting over to student body president, Dan Seigal. Seigal couldn't calm the screaming, angry crowd, who were yelling their outraged complaints about the destroyed plants and the eight foot fence. Kim and Gina were yelling along with the rest.

Finally, Siegal called out, "Let's take the park!" At that moment the police shut off the sound system and the crowd exploded. Roaring, they yelled "yes, let's take the park!" In one voice Kim and Gina bellowed, "we want the park," and raced down Telegraph to Haste street where they were met by a huge force of Berkeley and campus police guarding the fenced-off park site.

And the melee began. Someone opened a fire hydrant, shooting water over both police and protesters. Others attacked the fence, trying to break it down. Rocks and bottles flew through the air at the line of police, who then threw tear gas canisters at their assailants. Kim, who was soaking wet, clutched at his eyes with his free hand and turned away from the cloud of gas. He held on to Gina, who had pressed her face into his arm as they turned and ran up the street in the midst of the yelling, raging crowd. The police, in pursuit, their batons raised, shouted orders to "clear the area!" but more and more people pushed into the space in a swirling, boiling swarm of bodies. A car suddenly went up in flames and the air was now thick with smoke as well as tear gas. Gina was coughing, bent over, trying to breathe. Kim grabbed her hand and pulled her over to the edge of the throng where the air was clearer. He watched her closely, wondering if he should take her to the hospital. How dangerous was the gas? After a frightening few minutes Gina began to breath normally. "I'm OK now, Kim," she said, giving him a tremulous look.

As they remained in that spot on someone's lawn, trying to catch their breath, they watched as a stream of police cars, sirens howling, screeched to a halt at the street behind them. More sirens could be heard coming from all directions. Another raging stream of students and older residents burst into the crowd like a volcanic eruption, yelling at the police, shouting insults, the helmeted police in pursuit.

Kim eyed Gina, who was still breathing raggedly, her eyes red and tearing. He grasped her hand and they wormed their way through the crowd up the street to Telegraph Avenue, hoping to find cleaner air to breathe, all the time trying to avoid the batons of the police. When they reached Telegraph, Gina pointed to one of the police cars they passed. "Look, it's from the County Sheriff's department. They've called in more cops. Not just from Berkeley and the Highway patrol, and they're wearing those blue jumpsuits. They're the Blue Meanies, the guys who hurt people during the Third World protest."

It was then Kim saw the shotguns in the hands of deputies in blue jumpsuits, black boots and gloves. Then he heard the shots. Protesters screamed, shouted, threw rocks, bottles, whatever they could find. Cops in riot gear, helmets, shields and gas masks, slashed their batons, cracking heads and shoulders, shoving and dragging men and women toward the police vans. Kim, trying to keep hold of Gina's hand, plunged into the wall of bodies, adrenaline pumping, fear overtaking his rage, desperate to escape the violence. Suddenly, his head exploded with pain. He'd been hit. He released Gina's hand to stop the flow of blood that poured down his face.

Gina screamed and held his arm, pulling him into a doorway, pointing to the the line of National Guardsmen marching down Telegraph, M1 rifles tipped with bayonets. Overhead he heard the sound of helicopters and then the explosions and clouds of more tear gas. With Kim's hand clapped to his bleeding wound, and making slits of his eyes to avoid the gas, he watched as the soldiers, bayonets pointing, marched forward, herding the yelling students before them. Gina tugged him deeper into the shop's doorway and sobbed into his shoulder.

Hank had been at the Lab's computer when his friend Scott tapped him on the shoulder. "Trouble on the campus again, Hank. At the park. I just listened to KPFA. Students are rioting. Big time."

Hank twisted in his chair and stared at Scott, knowing that Kim would be there, for sure. "What do they say?"

"Well, Governor Reagan decided to get tough—to stop the protests and rioting and takeover of state property. He ordered the State Highway Patrol to go to the park at 4 o'clock in the morning before anyone knew about it. The cops put up a big fence, tore out the plants. Students were furious and came out in droves. Just now Reagan called in the California National Guard."

Hank sucked in a quick breath. Shit. "Any arrests?"

"Yeah, protesters are being dragged into police vans. KPFA says over 6,000 people—students and Berkeley people—suddenly showed up. They're tangling with cops called in from all over. Sheriff's deputies are using shotguns. Some guy up on the roof on Telegraph—who was just watching—was hit. They think he might be dead."

"Those fucking bastards!" It was then Hank heard the unmistakable sound of helicopters circling overhead, sounding like they were in the midst of a war. Which they were, of course, in Vietnam, but not in Berkeley. He jumped up from his chair. Would Kim call home if he was arrested? Or hurt? He grabbed his briefcase. "I've got to get home. Scott, If anyone wants me tell them what happened." He raced to his car and within minutes he was on the way to Berkeley, circumventing the campus and park area. He caught sight of two helicopters circling low in the sky. As he pressed the gas pedal down, his anger accelerated. Reagan and the God damned cops were overreacting! And so were the students. Would it ever stop?

When Hank pulled into his driveway he noted Angela's Volvo parked in the garage and guessed that she'd heard the news and had also come home early. From inside the house he heard Angus barking and when he opened the door the dog greeted him, jumping joyfully. "OK, boy. I'm home. At least someone's happy." He dropped his briefcase on the table by the door and hurried into the living room. He could hear Angela's voice from the kitchen as well as that of a radio news announcer. When he walked into the kitchen she'd just hung up the phone. "Any news of Kim?" he asked, moving toward her, kissing her tense cheek.

"No. But on the radio they said that over a hundred protesters have been treated for serious injuries at local hospitals. And hundreds were arrested. I called Cowell and Alta Bates and Kaiser hospitals but Kim isn't listed. I hesitated to call the police."

"Let's hope he's holed up somewhere keeping out of the way. I thought he might call."

Angela stared at the phone, breathing rapidly. "Me too. What can we do!"

As she spoke, Hank heard a car drive into the driveway. He peered out the window. "It's Kim!" They both rushed out the back door, but Hank was startled to see a long-haired girl open the drivers' door and rush around to the passenger side of the car. He and Angela scrambled toward the VW, calling Kim's name. They could see his bloodied head, wrapped in a stained yellow scarf, lying back on the neck rest. Gina was pulling on his arm, attempting to move him. Hank leaned into the car and Gina stepped aside. "A cop hit him. Hard," she blurted. "He needs a doctor." She looked up at Hank, red-eyed, pleading, shocked. "He's afraid to go to the hospital. They might arrest him."

Hank took hold of Kim's shoulders. "Let's get him inside. We'll look at the wound and call our doctor." Gina nodded, and slumped back against the hood of the car while Hank and Angela tugged Kim from his seat and onto his feet. As he opened his eyes and took his first shaky steps he mumbled, "I'm OK, Dad, Mom. No big deal.

Chapter Six

Berkeley, May, 1969: A shaft of morning sunlight traced a square pattern on the braided rug next to the bed. Gina had been awake for a few minutes and could hear voices coming from downstairs. She sat up and reached for the robe at the foot of her bed and held it in her lap a moment, attempting to clear her head. Her brain had been racing. Images of glinting bayonets, sounds of tear gas canister bombs, and the sight of blood streaming down Kim's face kept up a constant replay. Would Kim be awake yet? The doctor had told him to stay quiet for a few days, but that the blow hadn't caused a concussion, thank God. Kim's mother had put him to bed in her studio downstairs, so he would be easy to care for during the day. He'd been exhausted, of course, and the doctor had given him something to ease the pain. He'd fallen asleep before he'd finished the cup of broth his mother had given him.

But now it was time for her to get up. She was anxious to see how Kim was doing. Climbing out of bed, she glanced around the room, a guest room in Kim's parents' house. They'd insisted she stay here. Since Governor Reagan had declared a state of emergency, the campus and streets around it were being patrolled by police, sheriffs and National Guardsmen. Classes had been suspended and the libraries were closed. Yesterday evening she'd called her co-op, which was within the patrolled area, and her housemates had told her how from their window during the mayhem they could see National Guardsmen and police chasing students down the street. Between booms of tear gas canisters exploding they could hear the students' screams as they ran from the bayonet-tipped rifles and slashing batons.

The windows had to be closed tightly to keep out the clouds of tear gas the helicopters had dropped around them. Now the Guardsmen were stationed on their street below. They could watch them from their windows. And there was going to be a curfew, but they didn't yet know the schedule. Everyone worried about when they'd take their finals and write their papers with the libraries closed.

Gina shook away these dismal thoughts, slipped on the robe and tied the belt. The bathroom was across the hall, and Kim's mother had found her a toothbrush, left a towel for her and loaned her a night gown and bathrobe. She was a warm, welcoming woman, an artist. Angela was her name. She taught art at Contra Costa college. Kim' s father was nice, too, though quieter. They'd both been so concerned about Kim, and for her, too, wanting to hear what she'd seen and heard during the confrontation between the students and the police. And they were deeply shocked and angry at the police use of shotguns and of Reagan's calling in the National Guard.

After using the bathroom and getting dressed, she glanced at her reflection in the mirror and ran a comb through her long hair. Her skin was paler than usual with a bluish cast under her eyes, but she looked more or less alive. Angela had loaned her a clean shirt to replace the blood-spattered one she'd worn yesterday. She'd also taken her yellow wool sweater to wash, which also had been stained with Kim's blood. Descending the stairs, Gina followed the sounds of voices that were coming from what turned out to be the kitchen. Kim's parents were both at the table in the roomy kitchen's center. Angela rose to greet her and Angus, Kim's dog, whom she'd met yesterday, wagged his tail and sniffed at her shoes. "Did you sleep all right, Gina?" Angela asked.

Gina smiled. "Yes, I did. In spite of everything. I just crashed. And did Kim sleep through the night? Is he OK?"

Angela nodded. "He's still asleep. I checked on him a few minutes ago and he's breathing easily and his skin color looks good. But come, Gina, sit down and have some breakfast." She gestured to a chair at the kitchen table and then poured coffee for her and re-filled Hank's cup and her own.

After a smiling greeting to Gina, Hank returned to his newspaper. Glancing at her, he said, "well, it looks as though we're in a war zone. Reagan has sent in 2,700 National Guard troops to patrol the campus area and stop any demonstration or students gathering."

"And what does the paper say about the people who were shot?"

Hank shook his head, giving Gina a solemn look. "One man died, and another may be blinded. They were using '00 buckshot to fire at people."

Gina slowly picked up her coffee cup. Angela touched her shoulder. "Gina, scrambled eggs? Toast?"

Gina nodded, but the sound of gunshots still echoed in her head. "Thanks, Mrs. Bardot." As she sipped her coffee, she thought of how terrified she'd been when she was guiding Kim to the campus parking lot to find his car. She'd tied her scarf around Kim's bloody wound to stop the bleeding and ducked into the book store when the owner unlocked his door. He'd shown them the back door to the shop and they'd fled into the alley and then zigzagged their way to the parking lot, all the while hearing gunshots, explosions of tear gas, and circling helicopters. She'd gripped Kim's arm, guiding him, her own eyes stinging and streaming with tears, gasping for breath as they ran. Kim had permitted her to hold his arm, to keep him up on his feet, and when they reached his car he'd had the presence of mind to fish out the car keys from his pants pocket. And what a relief it was to get by the line of Berkeley police blocking Bancroft. She'd just waved at them and kept going.

Now she realized Angela was setting a plate of scrambled eggs and toast before her and taking her seat beside her. "Gina, I think we need to thank you again for bringing Kim home. From here at the house we could hear the helicopters and the explosions. We were so afraid he'd be badly hurt," and she paused, "or arrested." She and Hank exchanged troubled glances.

Hank put down the newspaper. He gave Gina a lingering look. "Yes, and thanks to your First Aid he didn't lose too much blood, and your quick action prevented his arrest—which might have had unfortunate consequences." Angela had risen from her chair and briefly touched Hank's arm.

At that moment the telephone on the kitchen counter rang. Hank jumped up to answer it. "Michael hi," he said, "yes, he's home. He's still asleep but seems to be OK." After a pause he was nodding, "good, Michael, we'll see you this afternoon. OK. Drive carefully." He hung up the phone and turned to Angela. "You heard that? "Michael wants to see Kim, hear his story, talk to him, but now I have to get to work. He gave Angela a quick kiss. "You're staying home today, right?"

She nodded. "Of course. Sandra is taking my three o'clock class. I'll be watching Kim—like Doctor Norton told us, but can you avoid police or guard check points?"

"Sure. I'll just have to avoid the streets around the University. And I'll show my I.D. if I'm stopped. Bye, Gina. See you later." He picked up his briefcase and jacket he'd placed on one of the chairs, waved and went out the back door. Gina finished off her eggs and toast, watching Angela, noting the distress in her gray eyes.

The traffic was picking up as Michael, in his '61 Ford coupe, approached the San Francisco/Oakland Bay bridge, but the sun was shining brightly, casting sparkling streaks of light on the waves undulating in the bay. He usually enjoyed this drive home. He could already catch a glimpse of the Campanile against the still-green hills behind it. It looked so peaceful, but he knew the U.C. campus was a battlefield—like Stanford had been the last few weeks, only worse, from what he'd read in the newspaper, and he was worried about Kim. Dad had said he was not seriously hurt, not to worry, but Kim had turned into a such a radical. Eventually, he was bound to get hurt, maybe kicked out of school. And then what? Canada? Prison? Vietnam? Would it be possible to to talk to him, tell him to cool it, tone down his militant talk and behavior? Kim used to listen to him, but since he became an FSM member and then got into this people's park stuff he stopped listening. Instead he preached—like his own housemates, Julie and Alistair, spouting rhetoric, repeating irritating catchwords heard at meetings or read in the leftist press.

When he drove into the family driveway, he noted the three cars belonging to his parents and Kim. Everyone must be home—including Angus, who dashed down the driveway from the back of the house, and barked at him joyfully, jumping around him as he climbed out of the VW. "Good to see you, Angus," Michael said, laughing, leaning down to scratch the dog's ears. After grabbing the small duffel and his briefcase from the car, he ran up the steps to the front door which, as usual, was unlocked. Before he could close the door behind him he heard his mother's voice. "Michael, wonderful! You're home."

Michael grinned. Mom always sounded surprised to see him even when she was expecting him. He dropped his duffel and briefcase next to the door, and greeted her with a hug. Peering over her shoulder into the living room, he saw Dad and Kim and a pretty girl with long, light brown hair. Kim was propped up on the couch with pillows behind his bandaged head and the girl sat close beside him.

Dad rose from his chair, and he and Michael embraced. "It's good to see, you, Michael. It's been a while. Are you OK? Surviving the excitement over there at Stanford?"

"Sure, Dad." Michael then moved toward Kim and leaning down, grasped his shoulder. "How are you, Kim? It looks like you've barely survived the uproar here in Berkeley."

"Oh, I'm OK. Just a little knock on the head, but I'll live!" Kim then turned to Gina and reached for her hand. "Gina, this is my big brother, Michael. Michael, Gina." They exchanged greetings and Michael settled in a nearby chair."

Angela, who had been standing in the living room doorway excused herself. "I need to start dinner, but Michael, I want to hear what's going on at Stanford. I'll be back in a minute."

He nodded, thinking that she looked strained. And why wouldn't she? Kim looked terrible. Beside the thick bandage around his head, one of his eyes was swollen and the skin around it a sickening greenish blue. Why did he need to be such a rebel? He then eyed

33

Gina, who was getting up from her place next to Kim. An attractive girl, for sure. A very attractive girl. After giving Kim a quick glance, Gina quietly said that she wanted to help and followed Angela into the kitchen. After she left, the three men eyed one another silently. Michael didn't know what to say to Kim, except to sympathize with his wounds. Maybe the hit on his head would knock some sense into him, cause him to think prudently for a change—to consider his future.

Hank shifted in his leather easy chair and gave Michael a sharp look. "So, Michael, from what I hear, Stanford students and faculty have joined the crusade. The Trustees decided to stop classified research for the government and divest the Research Institute from the university. What will that mean for you?"

"I wish I knew. Some of my professors are talking about leaving— going to SRI—and taking their grants with them. I don't know what they'll do with us grad students." He fished a cigarette from his shirt pocket and offered the pack out to Dad, then Kim, who shook his head.

After lighting Dad's and his own cigarettes, Dad looked up, his eyes with fatigue. He spoke quietly. "I assume you've finished your course work? Your grad school status is still OK?"

"Right. I managed to get my work finished and turned in— although, believe me, it's been almost fucking impossible with the lab being occupied these last two weeks."

Kim then spoke up. "So are you actually going to graduate?"

"Yeah, at least I think so. The administration building is in a mess at the moment, but my professors said they'd turned in grades for me—and they're good."

Kim gave him his one-eyed look, and almost with a sneer, said, "and did you stand around and watch as the cops beat up the students?"

"Kim," Michael said quickly, "listen, the cops didn't beat up the students until they started trashing the SRI annexe. I happened to be on campus when they cleared the administration building, but everyone left peacefully. Nobody was hurt."

Kim's one eye was accusing. "But you didn't take part in the protest!"

"For Christ sake, Kim, of course not. I need to graduate, go to grad school. Get my education so I have the skills to make a difference. And what good did your protests do? Did anyone listen to you? Did the war stop? No, it keeps on escalating! The casualties and atrocities mount every day. Have you watched TV? And it just gave Reagan the excuse to send in the National Guard and show the country how tough he is on radicals—and to shut down the school. What will happen to the graduating seniors if they can't take their finals or attend classes? The quarter is over. What will they . . ." Michael then noticed Mom standing in the doorway, staring at him, her eyes clouded, pained. His words dwindled away. Shit. Kim had been badly injured. He was supposed to be recuperating. This was not the time to confront him. Slowly rising from his chair, Michael took a deep breath, and attempted a conciliatory smile. "Kim, let's thrash this all out later when you're feeling better. I'm sorry. Really. It's just that so much is going on—people getting killed, hurt, sent to jail, programs being shut down. We'll talk later, OK?"

Kim looked at Mom, then Michael, and with a reluctant nod, mumbled, "OK."

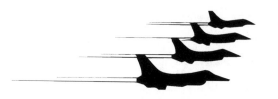

Chapter Seven

Berkeley, May, 1969: It was mid-morning, Sunday, three days after Bloody Thursday, as it was being called, and Gina and Michael were helping Kim move back into his own quarters. The bandage on his head had been taken off as the doctor had ordered. The two-inch strip of stitches on his scalp was now open to the air, and quite visible since the thick thatch of curly hair surrounding it had been shaved. The swelling had gone down from his blackened eye and the skin under it had faded to a bluish yellow.

Gina was still staying in the Bardots' guest room. She'd called her parents and told them where she was and not to worry. Angela had spoken to her mother, which seemed to calm her. Michael had also decided to stay longer. The Stanford semester was over, he'd told her. He would now have a break before the summer session. The computer lab, where he still had a job, wouldn't need him until then. Actually, she'd been enjoying Michael's company. Since that first day, when he'd been so stern with Kim, he'd been fun to talk to. He was a straight kind of guy, but he wasn't boring.

Gina's major concern at the moment was how she needed to finish papers for two of her classes. Unfortunately, the books and notes she needed were in her room at the co-op on Bancroft. This morning she'd phoned her housemate, Nadine, who'd told her the Guards were stopping people if they were in groups of more than three or four—and that she was afraid to go out on the street. It was then that Gina had decided to accept Angela's invitation to stay with them a few days longer. Sooner or later, Reagan would be calling off the troops, but until then she felt safer here. But she really needed to get her stuff. She was considering asking Michael to drive her close to campus and walk her to her co-op. Kim was supposed to stay quiet for a few more days.

Now Kim was sprawled on his bed, his head leaning on his propped elbow. Gina had moved Kim's books from his night table and was arranging his medications. She held out one of the containers "This little one has the pain pills, to take if you need them, but no more than four in a day. The other one is the anti-biotic. . ."

"Yeah, I know. One every fucking six hours." He grinned. "I can read, you know. My brain is OK." He took hold of her hand and tugged her onto the bed. She perched on the edge of the mattress but reclaimed her hand. Was she fussing too much? Acting like his mother? She glanced briefly at Michael, who was moving toward the door. Kim then leaned back on the bed and gingerly rested his head on his pillow. "Thanks, you guys, for helping me move back into my room. And, Gina, I heard you talking to Nadine. Any news?"

"No. Except the Guards are everywhere. She can see them from her window. The campus is still shut down. And all the libraries. And I need to get my books and notes. What about you, Kim? Do you have everything you need to finish your papers, or study for Finals?"

He groaned. "Christ, I don't know." He pointed to the confused piles of papers and books on the desk in front of the window. I sure as hell don't feel like working on any of it."

Michael, who was leaning against the wall next to the door, gave Kim a troubled look. "What about Finals? Did your professors assign anything before things shut down?"

"Two of them gave us take-home finals, but the other two didn't tell us anything. I really don't know what we're supposed to do. Take an incomplete maybe? Make it up next quarter?"

Gina bit her lip, thinking what they were all unwilling to put into words. What would the draft board do? Would they accept an incomplete and grant him a student deferral? She glanced at Michael, hoping he would have an answer, but he'd opened the door as if he were leaving. As he did so Angus, the collie, came dashing inside, jumping on the bed, licking Kim's face. Laughing, Kim, fended him off and ordered him to get down. Angus merely moved to the bottom of the bed and made himself a nest in the comforter.

Gina reached over and scratched Angus behind his ears. "Well, Kim, Angus, it's time for me to face the troops on the Bancroft Ave front line. I really have to get my stuff." She turned to Michael. "Will you go with me?"

"Sure, Gina. Be happy to." He shot her a quick glance and went out the door. She leaned down to Kim and gave him a cautious peck on the cheek. "You should rest for a while now, Kim. See you later."

A shadow had crossed Kim's bruised face. "Be careful, Gina." and she could feel his eyes following her as she left the room and closed the door behind her.

Hank and Angela were on the redwood deck reading the Sunday paper when Michael and Gina stopped to tell them they were leaving. "Kim is resting a while after the excitement of moving," Gina said, "and Michael has offered to drive me close to campus. And to walk with me to my room on Bancroft. I need to get some stuff for school, and I'm afraid to walk there alone with those National Guards stopping people."

Michael gave a rueful smile. "I really don't know what sort of escort I'll be, but it could be interesting!"

Angela's forehead wrinkled with concern. "Gina, is it really necessary to do this? If you need clothes, I'm sure I can fix you up with something."

"Yes, I really have to. I have papers to write and a take-home final to do. And nobody seems to know how long this military occupation will go on. You've been so generous, taking me in like this, but it's not clothes I need, but my books and notes."

Hank rose from his deck chair. "Michael, take care."

"I will, believe me!" and he led Gina to his Ford.

Michael drove down the hill onto Shattuck and then up University to the edge of the campus where he found a parking spot. "Let's try going up Bancroft," he said, placing his hand lightly at Gina's back, moving forward. A pair of Guardsmen were standing by a wooden barrier crossing the entryway to the campus from University Ave.

Bancroft was also guarded. As they approached one of the guards, Gina edged closer to Michael. Her pulse had quickened. She could feel her heart thumping. Did she really need to do this? Could she face these soldiers again? She felt as if she could still smell the tear gas. Michael's hand remained touching the small of her back. She found that touch reassuring. She trusted him. He would know how to handle the soldiers. Now one of the guards was stopping their progress, blocking the sidewalk. He carried a rifle, but it wasn't tipped with a bayonet this time, and although he wore a helmet, the visor was up and she could see his young face and wide blue eyes. He didn't look much older than she was. He could be a Cal student.

"The university campus is closed." The Guard's tone was gruff, but he didn't make eye contact and she didn't believe he'd beat them up like the cops had—maybe. She tried not to stare at his rifle.

Michael stepped forward. "We're going to this student's residence to collect books she needs."

The guard eyed them both. "I.D's, please. Are you students here?"

Gina pulled her wallet from her jeans' pocket and handed him her student body card and driver's license. Michael held out his Stanford I.D. "I'm a student at Stanford, visiting my parents who live in Berkeley. Miss Olivetti is staying at my parents house until classes start again." He then handed over his drivers' license which contained his Berkeley address."

The young guard studied the I.D's and scrutinized their faces. He handed the cards back then pointed to the opening in the barricade. "Proceed, but you are hereby warned that gatherings of more than three people within the guarded area is not permitted."

They quickly shoved their I.D's back into their pockets, stepped around the barrier and walked briskly up the street. Gina clutched at Michael's hand, trying to calm her breathing. Michael was scanning the street. "There's another group of guards at the next corner."

Gina had already seen them. "I hope we don't have to be questioned again." She gave a nervous laugh. "I keep wondering if they'll bash me with their rifles!"

Michael squeezed her hand and smiled. "They won't, you know, unless you start running or throwing things at them."

"Which I'm not about to do!" But as she passed line of soldiers, she wanted to run. Instead she stared straight ahead and continued at the same pace as before. When they finally reached her co-op building they ran up the outdoor steps and with fumbling fingers Gina unlocked the door and they dashed inside. Michael slammed the door behind them.

"Thank God we got through." Gina cried. "Now I'll just get my stuff and let's get out of here." They raced up the stairs to her room to find three girls standing at the top of the stairs, their eyes wide with alarm. When they realized it was Gina, they laughed and hugged her, their beaded necklaces jingling, all talking at once. Gina quickly introduced Michael and they both escaped into her room. She grabbed a canvas duffel from her closet and rapidly stuffed books, papers, toilet articles—including her birth control pills—some underwear, two embroidered peasant blouses and a pair of jeans into it. Hesitating a moment, she dug into a drawer, and glancing to make sure Michael wasn't watching, she grabbed a small baggie of grass and shoved it in with the rest. She'd take some to Kim. He needed it. She pulled on her Mexican leather jacket, zipped up the duffel, and surveyed her room. "I think this is all I'll need, so let's split."

They retraced their steps to Michael's car without being stopped. The young soldier who had first questioned them watched them closely as they approached, but with what Gina considered was a casual air, stepped forward and moved the barrier allowing them to pass. Both Gina and Michael moved smartly as they strode by the soldier, looking neither to left or right, fixing their eyes straight ahead.

When they reached the car at last, Michael set down the duffel, fished out his keys and unlocked the door, but as he stepped back from stowing the bag and turned to Gina, he saw that she was leaning against the fender breathing rapidly, ashen faced, her hand held over her chest. He touched her gently on her arm. "Gina, are you OK? You're as pale as a ghost!"

"I just need to catch my breath. I was really scared back there."

First scanning the street, Michael then pointed to a coffee shop a few yards away. "Come on, let's get you some water—or coffee or something," and holding her arm, he guided her into the small cafe, where they sat across from each other in a red vinyl booth. After several gulps of ice water, then sips of coffee, Gina's breathing slowed and she seemed to relax a little. Michael sipped his coffee, his eyes fixed on hers. "Your color is returning," he said, setting down his coffee, smiling at her.

"I guess I was really scared. And there wasn't any real reason to be. The Guard was quite polite. I don't think he was used to being a soldier."

Michael raised his eyebrows and laughed. "Right. He's in the Reserve. He doesn't expect to have to fight. And I can't imagine he truly likes to point his rifle at pretty coeds."

"And they don't have to go to Vietnam?"

"No. They don't go to Vietnam. They're supposed to guard the U.S. All of us guys know that, and anyone who wants to avoid being drafted into the regular army considers volunteering for the Guard, but it's not easy to get accepted. You have to know somebody, somebody with clout with the government, or politics, or the Pentagon. I know guys from rich families who got in."

Gina sighed. "How unfair!"

Michael nodded. "Yeah. Right on."

Gina laughed. "You don't generally use hippie phrases, do you Michael?"

He grinned. "I guess I don't. I don't know what you call guys like me." He wondered what she really thought of him.

"Straight, conservative, not hip? Steady?" She sipped her water.

"OK, steady's good. I just want to finish school, get my Ph.D, find a good job. What about you, Gina? I don't even know what you're majoring in. How did you get caught up in this park business and the FSM? And I don't even know where you're from?" Kim had told him almost nothing about Gina, just that he'd only known her a month or so, that he met her making posters about the park project.

Gina gave him a long look and set down her coffee cup. "I went to school in Napa. My family has a vineyard and winery north of there. The Olivettis emigrated from the north of Italy in the early 1900's and have been there since. I'm majoring in biology, but take a lot of art courses, which is how I met Kim. OK?" She smiled and brushed a long strand of her light brown hair back over her shoulder.

He laughed. "OK!" As she spoke, her eyes became lively, filled with light. They were greenish blue with flecks of gold. He could imagine her in a Botticelli painting, like the ones he'd seen at the Ufizzi last summer—creamy skin, oval face, straight nose. No wonder Kim fell for her. He sighed. Lucky guy. "So, Gina, your family came from Italy. Have you been there?"

"Oh yes, several times. We have relatives near Torino and Milan. They're vintners like my father and grandfather."

"So your family continued an Italian tradition."

"Right. Very Italian. My father is strict, dominating—and Catholic. And he's a talented vintner. Our ranch is beautiful. It's not a big one, like many of them are, but he takes his grape-growing and wine very, very seriously." She gave a small laugh. "When I'm home I have to toe the line, though. He doesn't know a lot of things I've done, and I haven't told him about my going out with Kim."

Yes, lucky Kim. "Well, Gina, you look like you're feeling better. Kim will be concerned about you."

"Right. He'll worry. Let's go." She grabbed her jacket and slid out of the booth.

Michael dropped some coins on the table and they hurried to the car. As he drove back to his parents' house, Gina sitting beside him, he thought of his own trip to Italy. As much as he he'd been thrilled by what he saw there in places like the Ufizzi, he couldn't forget that Florence was the city where his girlfriend, Claire, had abandoned him for a handsome French sculptor. She'd been his first serious girlfriend, the first girl he'd slept with, and her betrayal had crushed him. They'd saved for the trip for months and had flown together on a charter flight to Milan. They met the sculptor, on the train to Florence and Claire fell for the guy immediately. Now he gave a sideways glance at Gina. Kim's girl. Hands off, Michael!

Chapter Eight

Berkeley, May,1969: Kim had finished his scrambled eggs and was lingering over his coffee. Gina sat next to him buttering her toast, and Michael was at the stove lifting the coffee carafe. Kim glanced at the kitchen wall clock. In another hour it would be time for his doctor's appointment. Seven days had passed since his wound had been treated and today he was scheduled to have the stitches taken out. Both Mom and Dad had left for work.

"More coffee, Kim?" Michael asked, bringing the coffee to the table.

"Sure. Thanks, Michael." Kim watched as Michael re-filled his cup then Gina's and his own and resumed his seat to drink his coffee. Kim wondered why Michael had been so quiet these last few days. When he first arrived he'd lectured him so passionately, angrily, about the dangers and futility of student protests, but then suddenly he'd become pleasant and helpful—and nice to Gina. It was probably Mom's doing. She was so worried about his head wound. Dad, too. Or maybe it was because Michael was too occupied worrying about his own status. "Michael," he said,"do you know anything more about what's going to happen to your grad program?"

Michael set down his coffee cup, spilling some on the table. He grunted and reached for a dish cloth to wipe up the spill. "Not really, Kim. I've called a couple of guys who are in the same situation, but they don't know much. The SRI relationship to the university still has to be worked out. I told you about Stanford divesting itself from SRI and classified research, much of it Vietnam war related stuff. Now it seems that faculty—physics professors, for instance—threaten to leave Stanford for the re-organized research institute and take their grants with them. It all has to be worked out by the Trustees, administrators and faculty. We just hope the entire physics department doesn't walk out. It leaves us grad students in a kind of limbo."

"What a fucking mess!" Gina said, her eyes fixed on Michael.

Michael nodded. "Right, Gina, a fucking mess."

Kim noted how Gina continued to gaze at his brother. He felt a stab of discomfort. He didn't want Gina to feel too sorry for his hard-working, ambitious big brother, who obviously wouldn't object too much to doing Vietnam war-related work. He glanced at the clock. He'd better get ready to go. He picked up his plate and cup and began to clear the table and load the dishwasher. "Gina, you'll come with me to the doctor's office, won't you?"

"Sure, Kim," and she joined him in the cleanup job.

Michael rinsed his coffee cup and then moved to the small radio on the counter and turned it on. "Let's see what KPFA has to say about what's happening on campus.

Kim gave a sharp laugh. "At least we don't hear helicopters yet."

The announcer was in the midst of a report. "*. . . it will be held at midday in Sproul Plaza. The memorial will honor James Rector, the man who was killed May 15, known as Bloody Thursday. The organizers have not received permission from the administration or the Alameda County Sheriff's department to proceed . . .*

Kim glanced at Gina, his eyebrows raised in an unspoken question. He intended to be there. His stitches will have been removed by then. He was feeling fine, why shouldn't they go? Gina stared back at him and shook her head. "If you're wondering if we should join the crowd, I'd say no. You can't take the chance, Kim. Your wound will still need to heal. You sure as hell don't need another hit on the head!"

He grinned. "We'll wear hooded sweatshirts."

Michael switched off the radio. "Kim, don't be stupid! Don't go anywhere near campus!"

Kim shrugged. "Fuck off, Michael. Don't lay that big brother shit on me. Come on, Gina!" and he tramped out of the room.

Gina hesitated a moment, shot Michael a quick look, then turned to follow Kim.

Gina sat in Doctor Norton's downtown Berkeley waiting room while Kim had his sutures removed. She'd been pondering over how she would persuade Kim not to attend the Memorial. She most certainly did not want to go with him. The brutality she'd witnessed on Bloody Thursday was etched so sharply in her memory, and she'd been so scared that day with Michael. Nothing had happened, really, but the sight of the Guards with their rifles had flooded her brain with a replay of the terrifying sounds and sights she'd experienced the day Kim was clubbed.

The door to the surgery opened and a beaming Kim appeared before her. He was struggling into his hooded sweatshirt, but before putting up the hood he turned his head toward her. "So, how does it look, Gina?"

She rose and examined his wound, pushing back the mass of thick curls to expose the shaved patch. "It looks good. It's still a little red around the edges, but it's not going to show, you know, as soon as your hair grows back."

"Yeah, well, let's get out of here. We don't want to miss the meeting."

"Kim, did the doctor say anything about your needing to take it easy? To stay quiet for a few days longer?"

"No. He said I was fine. The wound is healing nicely." He opened the door and within minutes he'd guided them out onto the street. "I think we can leave my car parked where it is and walk from here. OK?" and he took hold of her hand and led her briskly up Durant toward the campus.

Gina pulled back, slowing her steps. "Kim, I really don't want to go to the meeting. It will undoubtedly become violent. The Guards will swoop in again—and the sheriffs and police with their guns and clubs. And the tear gas."

"But Gina, we have to be there! We can't let those bastards get away with murder. They killed the poor guy, an innocent bystander.

We've got to protest, let our voices be heard. We're not cowards. I may refuse to fight in Vietnam, but I can sure as hell fight the establishment, the killers like Reagan and Nixon."

Gina continued to pull back. What could she say to stop him. For the millionth time she thought of the blood steaming down his face, dripping onto their shirts, the glazed expression in his eyes after he'd been hit.

By now they had entered the guarded area. Two Berkeley policemen were standing by the wooden barrier watching them. "The campus is closed. Are you students here?" one of them said gruffly. "Attending gatherings of more than three people is forbidden."

Gina considered turning away, but she saw that Kim was pulling out his wallet to show his student body card and ID. Kim shot her a quick glance. "Show him, Gina. Show him your cards." He then turned to the cops. "She's heading for her residence on Bancroft."

The policeman first scrutinized the cards, then their faces and with a bored look beckoned for them to enter. He moved the barrier and Kim grasped Gina's hand and tugged her forward. Reluctantly, she followed.

As they continued their brisk trek toward Sproul Plaza the numbers of Guards and County Sheriff deputies, the Blue Meanies, increased. Unlike the day Gina was here with Michael, the National Guards carried rifles with fixed bayonets. She began to shake. "Kim, let's turn back and go. I'm so scared."

He gripped her hand more tightly and shot her an impassioned look. "I can't go back. I have to fight. Show these bullies we're not shirkers."

"Kim, I'm sorry, but I can't go with you. I'm just too fucking scared!"

His wide gray eyes softened and he grasped her shoulders. "Gina, If you can't do it, it's OK. Why don't you go to your co-op and wait there with Nadine, and I'll come and get you when it's over. Your roommates will let you in." He pointed to the corner. "Turn onto Dana. Just tell the Guards you're going to your residence on Bancroft.

They've got to let you through. You have your I.D. You'll be OK. You hear!"

She nodded wordlessly, squeezed his hand and rushed off toward the corner. When she turned onto Dana, she looked back. Kim was watching her. She waved, straightened her back and strode toward the pair of Guards posted there. Kim had been correct. The Guard listened to her request to go to her residence, examined her I.D. card and gave her a sympathetic look. "Go quickly. It might get rough around here!"

Rough, she thought, beginning to shake again, but racing toward her refuge. What more, she asked herself, could she have said or done to stop Kim from joining the protesters? He'd been so determined, but so foolish. His wound was still healing.

When she turned on to Bancroft she was stunned to see a line of Guards stretching down the street, blocking access to the campus. They were armed with bayonet-tipped rifles and gas masks. She ran toward her clapboard house just a few yards down the street, mounted the steps and pounded on the door. She didn't have her keys. Wildly, she scanned the line of Guards, who stood tall and motionless. Hurry, she thought. Sweet Jesus ! Someone just has to be home. Finally, she heard footsteps running down the stairs and then Nadine's tremulous voice, "who is it?"

"It's me, Gina. Please, Nadine, let me in!" The door swung open and she dashed inside while a terrified Nadine slammed the door behind her. Then Gina heard the juddering sound of a helicopter swooping overhead—and the boom of a tear gas canister exploding. Soon they would feel the sting of the gas in their eyes and throats. "We have to close off the windows," Nadine screamed, and they raced up the stairs.

Michael parked his car in the driveway and quickly opened the Ford's back door for Angus to jump out. As he dashed up the steps to the front door of his parents' house, he glanced up at the helicopters swooping overhead. He'd just been in the hills, taking the dog for a run when he'd watched the helicopters fly in the direction of the campus and then a few seconds later smell the tear gas. Reagan's boys were at it again. And what about Kim?

When he opened the door he heard his mother calling him. "Michael, thank God you're home." She came running our of her studio. "You've seen the helicopters. I hoped you hadn't gone to the campus, but I wasn't sure."

"No, Mom, I took Angus for a run. And yeah, I sure saw the helicopters—and smelled the tear gas. More trouble. But did Kim come back from the doctor's?"

Angela gripped his arm. "No, and I called the doctor's office and Kim had left already. His receptionist said that his girlfriend was with him. Michael, I'm afraid he's gone to that Memorial for the man who was killed."

He put his arm around her shoulders, trying to calm her. "Maybe he has. I'd hoped he'd have more sense, but he's so angry. And for good reason, but Gina is with him. And she seems like she has a good head on her shoulders. Maybe she'll keep him from doing something stupid."

Angela sighed. "Maybe, but they're so young, so trusting and. . ." She was interrupted by the sound of the telephone ringing. Her hand went over her heart and she ran to the phone in the kitchen. "It's Gina," she said, clutching the phone, biting her lip as she listened. Michael watched as the color in Angela's face drained away. Then she nodded her head, "OK Gina, I'll put it on. And stay where you are. Take care!" She hung up the phone and reached to the radio and switched it on. She spoke rapidly, breathing hard. "Gina is at her house on Bancroft. Kim went on to the meeting. She couldn't stop him. There are hundreds—maybe thousands—of Guards armed with bayonets, cops, sheriff's deputies, and Gina has been listening to KPFA. It's horrible and we should listen."

Michael switched on the radio to KPFA and adjusted the sound. The reporter's voice sounded tinny. He was speaking on a phone from an apartment above Telegraph Ave and Durant, connected to the nearby radio station. He coughed as he spoke, and sounds of women screaming, men shouting, tear gas canisters exploding, and police sirens blaring created a fearful background to his breathless report. *"Protesters are being herded down the street by a line of gas-masked National Guards standing shoulder to shoulder, moving relentlessly forward. From the window where I'm standing, through the haze of tear gas, I can see the crowd being forced into a vacant lot on Durant. Two large blue buses are parked there and police—Berkeley police, I believe, as well as Sheriff's deputies, are pushing and dragging men and women into the buses. I don't see any beatings, just the slow march of the Guards with their bayonets and helmets glinting in the sunlight and the steady action of the cops.* Suddenly, the connection to the station must have broken, since an announcer took over and gave a reprise of the on-the-spot report and a summary of the events of the day.

Michael fixed his eyes on Angela. She was holding her hand over her mouth. Tears were welling in her eyes. What could he say to her? She would be imagining Kim's wounded head, his bruised face, fearing another hit—maybe a concussion this time—or worse. "Mom, you heard the guy say he saw no beatings. And anyway, maybe Kim wasn't in that trap. Maybe he got away."

Angela fished a Kleenex from the pocket of her tailored pants and blew her nose. "Maybe." Then she reached for the phone. "I'll call Hank. If Kim has been arrested we'll have to take care of it." She dialed a number, asked for Doctor Bardot, then whispered her thanks and hung up. "He's left the lab. He must be on his way home."

Good, Michael thought. Mom needed someone with her, but he really wanted to find Gina, get the whole story. It took him only a few seconds to riffle through the scraps of paper next to the phone, to find her phone number. He dialed and finally, she answered. "Gina, it's Michael. Are you OK? And what about Kim? We're really worried. Have you heard from him?"

"Michael, I'm OK. But I don't know about Kim. He went on to the meeting and said he'd come for me when it was over. But he hasn't turned up. I don't know what happened to him!"

"Gina, can you see anything from your window? Anything happening?"

"All I can see is a scattering of Guards. The rest left. And most of the protesters have vanished."

He could hear her voice shaking as she spoke. "Gina," he said, "I'd like to get you out of there. I could come for you, bring you here where you're safe."

She immediately stopped him. "But Michael, what if Kim comes and I'm not here."

"Leave him a note, or tell your housemates to give him a message."

"I don't know, Michael, and maybe the Guards won't let you through the barrier."

"I'll try, Gina. And maybe by the time I get there Kim will be there. OK?"

"OK," and she said, a catch in her voice. "Take care."

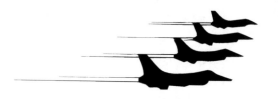

Chapter Nine

Berkeley, May,1969; As Hank drove home he heard the sound of a helicopter overhead. His eyes shifted to the sky above and he saw it circling, defiling the calm air with its juddering sound. Then he caught a glimpse of the Campanile shrouded in an ominously streaming cloud. Fucking tear gas! He could smell it and feel it in his throat. Here at this great university. God damn that Reagan. While he continued driving up the hill, he turned his attention to the broadcast on his car radio which was now reporting from outside the Alameda County Sheriff's facility, the Santa Rita jail. *Busloads of protesters, most of them young, are being herded into the grounds by armed guard. It's been reported that over 400 have been arrested.*

Hank's ribcage tightened. Kim could be among them. Would he have enough sense to keep his mouth shut? But he suspected that Kim would be speaking out, struggling. God damn. He was proud of the boy for his idealism but despaired for his survival. Now he turned into his driveway and hurried into the house where he heard the TV blaring from the living room. He found Angela on the couch, her attention riveted to the screen. He stopped in the middle of the room, transfixed by what he saw, ignoring Angus, who had run toward him. On the screen a blurred shot was shown of a line of disheveled young men descending from a bus and being shoved and jabbed into the prison yard by blue uniformed prison guards. The announcer reported that a witness who declined to be identified had entered the Santa Rita compound with a concealed camera and had snapped the picture and then escaped, mingling with the crowd of residents who had gathered to protest the Guards and police action.

Angela jumped up from the couch, anxiety etched on her face. "I still haven't heard from Kim. I tried to call Sana Rita, but they're not taking calls about the arrests." He reached for her and held her a few moments before she spoke again. "Michael has gone to fetch Gina, to bring her here. They should be here soon."

With his arm around her waist, he fixed his eyes on the television again, hoping for another showing of the Santa Rita scene. Maybe he'd pick out Kim in the jam of victims, but instead a Tide commercial flashed on. Angela moved to the television set and turned down the volume. "They've been showing that Santa Rita shot several times. There seems to be nothing new. Reporters aren't being allowed in the facility, but they say that one of the Chronicle reporters was arrested along with the protesters."

As Hank stood, motionless, paralyzed, staring at the stupid box of soap shown on the screen, he felt utterly useless. How could he help his son? What could he do to mitigate the damage done by Kim's actions? He took a deep breath and moved quickly to the phone. He'd call their lawyer, a man he'd known since his OSS days. He quickly searched their phone book for the number, but when he dialed, the line was busy. As he hung up he exchanged looks with Angela. "Half of Berkeley will be calling him. Maybe we should go to Santa Rita and see what we can find out."

Santa Rita: The gravel on the asphalt dug into Kim's cheek and hurt like hell, but that fucking guard had screamed at them to lie still, face down, their heads turned to the left, their arms at their sides. "Don't move until I tell you to! No talking!" He wanted desperately to move but when the guy next to him had lifted his head, a guard in a blue jumpsuit jabbed at him with his stick. His wound throbbed and he knew he must protect his head. He'd tried to keep his sweatshirt hood up, but a guard had yanked it down as he jogged through the gate into the yard. He didn't dare pull it up again. He'd obey orders, keep his head down. These Blue Meanies were brimming with hate. A lot of them were Vietnam vets. To them he was a draft dodger and a coward and deserved to be punished.

His neck ached and he strained his eyes attempting to inspect his surroundings. The bodies of the men around him, stretched out, twitching, but remaining like so much garbage, made the scene surreal. He could hear the guards tramping on the asphalt, looming large when they approached, tapping their riot sticks against their shiny black boots. Then when he thought he couldn't possibly keep his face in that position a moment longer the guard yelled, "now, turn your heads to the right! And keep still. Don't none of you move!"

Kim lost track of how long he lay there. Every twenty minutes or so the guard screamed for them to turn their heads to the other side. After what seemed like hours, and he later found that it had been two and a half hours, a few names were called. Twenty minutes or so later he heard his own name yelled out. "OK, you guys, get on your feet! Line up!" He and eight others were shoved, stiff and limping, into one of the buildings surrounding the yard to be booked. After giving his name, age etc, he was told what his charge was. "Misdemeanor. Failing to disburse and unlawful assembly." They were then returned to the yard and ordered to "get the hell back on the ground!"

After another long hour they were marched into the barracks and ordered to sit on the bunks or on the floor. Kim sat cross-legged on the wooden floor. His head pounded and he struggled to keep his eyes open. Suddenly, he realized the men were cheering. He stared toward the door where four well-groomed men were entering the crowded room. "We're lawyers from the People's Park Defense Committee" one of them called out." Again the men whooped and cheered. "We've brought your bail forms. Be sure to list the telephone numbers to be called. We'll be working through the night to arrange your bail. Good luck." and they passed out the forms and left.

At 11 p.m. Kim heard his name called again. He and seven others struggled onto their feet and were marched into another building. "Face the wall!" a guard snarled. "Get everything out of your pockets. Take off your belt." and he jabbed at Kim. "And you, you draft dodger, get out of your tennis shoes." After he was told to "put your garbage back in your pockets and put on your shoes," another man stapled a band with his name and serial number onto his wrist. When Kim's thumbprint was smudged and he had to do it over, the man glared at him. "Got to get 'em right, you know, for the FBI."

Kim looked up. "The FBI?"

"Hell, we're goin' to keep track of you troublemakers. We're goin' to enforce the McCarran act and put you bastards in concentration camps. OK, next!" and he waved to the next man in line. Kim could feel the hate spewing from the man. He looked away, knowing he must clamp a cap on the volcano of rage that threatened to erupt. This was not the place to speak out.

After mug shots were taken they were marched back to their barracks for several more hours. Kim ached from head to toe and was drugged with the desire to sleep, but the blue-uniformed guards screamed at them to sit up and shut up. When finally he glimpsed the gray light of dawn outside the barred windows, they were all marched into the mess hall and fed breakfast. As Kim swallowed his oatmeal he could barely keep his head up, but when the guard yelled at him to "sit up straight! eyes straight ahead" he sat up straight. "And next time you riot," the guard yelled, "remember this place! And wait 'till the boys get back from Nam. They'll know how to handle you idiots." With his eyes straight ahead, Kim drank his weak coffee, wondering when he'd get to make the one phone call the lawyers had promised or find out if his bail had been posted.

When he'd almost finished his oatmeal, a guard burst through the door and yelled. "Anyone here want to go home?" They all yelled a loud YES! "Then do as I tell you and run out to the gate and line up by twos. We're going to do some military drill! You'll be one step above the others when you finally get drafted." And he kept them running. "Faster. OK, halt! Alright, you creeps, I'm goin' to ask you something. I'm goin' to ask you who do we love? And you're goin' to shout out the Blue Meanies!" He paused, his eyes raking the line of men. "OK, who do we love?" The response could barely be heard. "OK, you jerks, you better shout it out or we'll run up and down this yard all day" He held his riot stick high in the air. "So, who do we love?" and the men shouted loud and clear, "the Blue Meanies."

Snickering, the guards opened the gate. "OK, you draft dodgers, get outta here!!"

As Kim stumbled through the gate into the crowd of people waiting, his heart gave a lurch when he saw Hank and Michael waving at him. Rushing forward, he fell into their embrace. "Dad, Michael—am I glad to see you! Let's get the hell out of here." With Hank holding one arm and Michael the other, they led him to Hank's car.

Angela and Gina were waiting by the door when Hank hauled Kim up front steps, his arm around Kim's shoulders. Michael hovered close behind, making sure he didn't fall. Hank could feel the boy's exhaustion at each step up. When they reached the porch, Angela rushed forward and threw her arms around Kim, murmuring incoherent phrases of sympathy and concern. Gina remained by the door, tears welling in her eyes, staring at Kim with shock. Hank gave Kim a closer look and noted the grime and sweat on his bruised face, the inky shadows under his eyes. His hair was a bird's nest tangle, his jeans and sweatshirt were stained with black dirt—and he stank. The boy needed a bath and sleep.

Angela clung to Kim's arm, guided him into the kitchen and with her hands on his shoulders gently pushed him into a chair. "You look a mess, Kim, but before you get into the shower and go to bed, I need to have a look at your wound. Did they beat you again?" Her voice trembled as she spoke.

"No, Mom," Kim croaked. "I kept my mouth shut and did as I was told. They hated me. Never in my life have I felt such hatred! We were just a bunch of draft dodgers and they despise us."

Angela carefully poked into the mass of curls on Kim's head, scrutinized his scalp, then nodded to Hank that the wound was OK. The tense muscles in Hank's back relaxed a little. Kim had kept his mouth shut for once and avoided being beaten. Maybe the boy had some sense after all, and maybe his arrest would not be noticed by the FBI or the NSA.

"And Dad," Kim added, "they didn't tell us anything. Like about our bail or what would happen to us next. In the car you tried to tell me about the bail, but my brain wasn't working. So did the Park Committee lawyers get hold of you?"

"Yes, they called around 3 A.M. Earlier your mother and I had driven to Santa Rita as soon as we heard on the radio about the arrests, and Gina had said you hadn't turned up at her residence, as you had promised. We were told then that the lawyers would probably be calling us if you had given them our phone number—so we went home and waited."

Angela touched Kim's cheek, "and we waited and waited, Kim. I was so worried about your head wound, scared that you had been hit again. Finally the lawyer called, but he didn't know what your condition was, just that you needed someone to come up with bail, and that you would probably be arraigned Monday."

"Monday," Kim mumbled, his eyes half-closed.

Gina, who had been standing next to Michael, pale and silent, stepped to Kim's side. "Kim, you can talk later. You need some sleep. Or do you need something to eat?"

"Yeah, I'm falling asleep right here. No, I couldn't eat."

Michael then reached forward and placed his hands on Kim's shoulders. "Come on, brother, let's get those filthy rags off and get you in the shower."

Gina moved to the door. "I'll go get him some clean clothes from his room."

Angela nodded to Gina while watching Michael lead Kim to the bathroom next to her studio. "And Michael, after his shower put him to bed in my studio." She turned to Hank. "I can keep tabs on him, make sure he's OK. And I sure won't be doing any work today!"

Hank went to her and drew her close. "No. Nobody will be doing any work. We'll all need to sleep. And, darling, maybe Kim's arrest won't be noticed. Too many other kids were caught in the net."

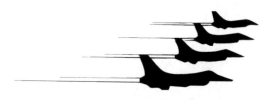

Chapter Ten

Berkeley, May, 1969; Michael leaned back in the canvas deck chair and gazed out at the bay. The sky was tinged with stripes of pink and orange as the sun began its descent over San Francisco. He picked up the book that lay face-down on his lap, but instead of reading, glanced at Gina, who was working at the redwood table next to him. She was frowning, her hand gripping her pen tightly as she wrote. He watched as she stretched her neck and tossed down her pen. He liked to watch her. Her face and eyes were so expressive, and her neck so graceful. If she weren't Kim's girl, he'd make his move, but that was something he would not do.

"I'm too exhausted to think!" she said, suddenly, reaching for her coffee cup. "Damn the Finals." She took a quick swig of coffee then shoved the cup away. "It's cold!

Michael smiled. "Shall I make more coffee?"

"No thanks, Michael, I'd get the jitters, for sure. I still haven't recovered from seeing Kim this morning. He looked so utterly defeated, so squashed. I could use some grass right now, but your parents would object if they caught a whiff of it. I really don't want to upset them. They've been so generous."

"Yeah, Dad would hit the roof. He says marijuana is illegal and he doesn't want it on his property, although I know Kim smokes in his room sometimes."

"I guess Kim is still asleep. I wonder if we should wake him up."

"Let him sleep, poor guy." Michael opened his book, but didn't take his eyes off Gina. She had such an intriguing face and now that she was so concerned about Kim it expressed depth, character. Botticelli would love her.

Footsteps on the steps to the deck caused him to turn away from Gina's face, to see Kim trudging toward them. He carried a thick sandwich in one hand and a coffee cup in the other.

Gina jumped up. "You're awake, Kim. How do you feel?" She pushed aside the papers scattered on the table, making room for him, and dragged over another chair.

He grinned. "Terrible, but a hell of a lot better than I did this morning." He set his cup on the table, touched Gina's arm and plunked down on the chair. He gave Michael a sharp glance, then looked at Gina. "So what have you guys been up to while I was rotting in jail?"

Gina laughed. "Worrying about you, Kim."

He bit into his sandwich, and then glancing at Gina said, "so the last time I saw you, you were going to your co-op. So what happened?"

"I stayed there until most of the National Guards had left. Then Michael phoned and came to get me. He'd found your extra car keys, and I drove your car here.'

After another quick glance at Michael, Kim took a sip of coffee and gazed out at the bay. "Jesus, it's good to be out of that place, smell the fresh air, look at the big sky—and he tilted his head back to look up. "And no helicopters. Has it been quiet today?"

Michael nodded. "But the troops are still on campus. Berkeley residents are furious, though, and are demanding they leave. They have a city permit for a peaceful march on Memorial day—to protest Reagan's occupation of the city. It should be interesting. But, Kim, you're not going to join the march, I hope."

"I guess it depends what happens at the arraignment."

Gina shot him a worried look. "Could you go to jail?"

Kim took a deep breath. "I guess it's not impossible. Those fucking Blue Meanies would get their jollies if we all went to jail. They sure hated us."

Michael leaned forward. "But the judge won't hate you. And Reagan won't be there. And there are so many of you." He grinned. "The jail's not big enough."

"But, Kim," Gina said, her eyes shadowed, "you haven't told us what happened to you in Santa Rita—except that the guards were bursting with hatred—and that they didn't let you sleep."

Michael fixed his eyes on Kim, noting that he was obviously reluctant to talk about it, but after taking a deep breath he finally mumbled a few details, like being kept face down on the gravelly asphalt for over three hours and being forbidden to move or talk.

Gina reached out and placed her hand on his. "How awful, Kim. Thank God it's over and bail was posted."

They were interrupted by Hank, who had just walked out the dining room French doors onto the deck. "So, Kim, you're awake. How do you feel?" He placed his hand on Kim's shoulder and gave him a close look. "You still look a little worse for wear, but you're all in one piece, at least. No blood this time."

"No, no blood," Kim said, with a wry smile.

Gina jumped up from her chair and dragged another to the table for Hank. "Kim was just telling a little about what happened at Santa Rita."

Kim frowned. "There's not much to tell, really."

Michael watched as Hank and Kim exchanged intense looks. He expected Dad to begin an interrogation, but he remained quiet, shifting in his chair. An awkward pause caused them all to move an arm or to cross their knees or ankles. Dad finally spoke."I was told there were over two hundred men in the section you were in. Your bail was posted at $500. The Park Committee lawyers arranged it all, and they'll be there at your arraignment Monday. You're to appear at 10A.M. The lawyers will speak for you. I doubt if you will have the opportunity to speak for yourselves, which in your case, Kim, is good, as far as I'm concerned. The less attention you get the better."

Kim stared at him. "Why is that, Dad? Haven't you raised us to speak out against injustice, and isn't what our country is doing to Vietnam an injustice?"

"Perhaps, but if you want your voice to be effective you need to choose the time and place to speak out."

Kim's jaw clenched and his gray eyes sparked in defiance. "Maybe it's time to stop speaking and start acting. Like the Panthers or SDS. With a big bang!"

Michael caught his breath. Kim was being weird. He watched Hank's expression harden, close down, then suddenly change. He slowly rose and with his eyes fastened on Kim's spoke slowly. "Kim, you're angry as hell at the cops, the jail guards, and your government. You've been treated harshly these last few days, have felt what it's like to be despised, hated. But before you decide to act as you say, think carefully. You have your entire life before you. And you have a family." He turned toward the house, and over his shoulder said, "if you're hungry come on in to supper. Angela is rustling up something to eat," and he went through the French doors into the house.

Still watching Kim, Michael stood up. "Well, come on, Kim. Maybe you need to eat something. You sure need to get more sleep. You've had a really rough deal."

Kim just glared at him.

Gina then sprang up and began to gather her books and papers. "Well, I don't know about you, Kim, but I'm hungry. And before you start throwing bombs you better get some food in your belly. Come on, dude," and she put her arm around his shoulders.

The frown melted and Kim gave her a tired smile. "Yeah, I guess I am hungry. And it's getting chilly out here." He slowly rose, took hold of Gina's hand, and they walked into the house.

On Monday, three days later, Angela and Hank waited outside the Alameda County Courthouse while Kim attended his arraignment along with 400 other protesters. The courtroom was overflowing, and visitors had not been allowed to enter. As they waited they were surrounded by a crowd of people, parents, perhaps, Angela speculated, or close friends of the prisoners. She and Hank had found an unoccupied bench in the park-like enclosure in front of the building. They both kept their eyes focused on the ornate double doors leading into it. They'd been waiting over an hour and Angela expected to wait much longer. How would the court process so many prisoners?

Angela thought about how Kim had been so quiet that morning, sober, obviously anxious—and for good reason. He was so innocent, really. He thought he'd been virtuous, speaking out against the war, believing the park was a worthwhile gesture, and never expected to be thrown in jail because of it. Or, she supposed, he didn't believe that he, Kim, would be punished for it. He'd been raised in a cocoon of Berkeley civility. But maybe it was her fault. He was her baby, the sunny one, the artist. Michael had always been more serious, always a little cautious.

But Reagan had surely overreacted. Who would've predicted that students would be subjected to such brutality—here in California—in 1969. These students didn't deserve to be confronted by armed police and National Guards, and from what she'd read in the Chronicle, their harsh treatment in the Santa Rita jail. The reporter had published his experience after his arrest. Kim hadn't wanted to talk about it, but the story appeared on their front doorstep when the paper was delivered Saturday morning. That same paper had news about the strike settlement at San Francisco State. The strikers had won. The Blacks got their Black Studies department, the Third World people got their Ethnic Studies department and places for 400 non-white students would be available in the Fall semester. Kim had read the news and had spoken bitterly about how the protests at Berkeley had failed so miserably.

She glanced at Hank. He was scanning the surrounding crowd of anxious parents and comrades. He'd been so upset about Kim, worried about his student deferral, his misdemeanor charge, concerned about his head-wound. As was she, of course, but somehow she didn't believe Kim would be convicted and sent to jail. They couldn't do that to him!

While Angela and Hank waited at the courthouse, Michael and Gina waited at their home. Carrying a cup of coffee, Gina walked into the Bardot's living room to join Michael, who was sprawled on the couch, his face hidden by the morning Chronicle. Balancing her coffee cup, she settled into a leather armchair, kicked off her sandals and folded her jeans-clad legs under her. She glanced at Michael, so absorbed in the newspaper, so quiet. Either he had steady nerves, or he believed Kim would be released. Or maybe he figured Kim deserved to go to jail. She sighed, wishing the telephone would ring. Angela had promised to phone if there was any news. "I wonder how long we'll have to wait. They've been gone almost two hours."

Michael looked up from the newspaper. "No telling. I guess it depends how they handle the cases. As a group or individually. It could take hours." He paused, his brown eyes fixed on hers. "But, Gina, even if he's convicted the time served will be short. Maybe just a few weeks."

She stared at him. "But what will happen to his draft deferral if he's not in school?

He put down the newspaper. "I don't know, really, but maybe they'd give him an extension and let him register for the next quarter."

Gina took a long gulp of her coffee, set it down on the side table, and shifted in the chair. She fingered the string of blue beads at her neck and glanced again at the phone. How she wished it would ring. If Kim had to go to jail, maybe the University wouldn't want him back. She sighed, exchanged looks with Michael, then gestured to the newspaper. "So anything new about the arrests—or the troops?"

"Nothing new, really, just that the arraignment is scheduled for this morning, and the Memorial day committee was granted permits for their march. Reagan agreed to withdraw the troops from campus, but they're bivouacked at the park, guarding it. It says participants are to meet at Memorial Stadium and march to the park."

Gina fastened her eyes on Michael. "How about you, Michael? Will you join them?"

"I think I will. It's being organized by responsible citizens. They're fed up with the occupation. Some people who were just out shopping on Shattuck were arrested and sent to Santa Rita. If they were treated like Kim was treated you'll know that Berkeleyans will be livid."

She thought about the Guards, their bayonets, the gas masks, all so terrifying. What a relief it would be if the Guards were gone. And maybe she'd go on the march, too. She could go back to her co-op. Staying here with Kim and Michael had been rather fun, but what about Finals? She turned again to Michael. "If the Guards have been withdrawn from campus I wonder if they'll open the libraries and go ahead with Finals week—and Commencement."

Michael shuffled the pages of the paper and shook his head. "Not mentioned, but you'll be sure to hear if that happens."

"I guess so." Gina untangled herself from the chair and gazed out the big window facing the street. The sun was shining and the sky was a brilliant blue. How horrible if Kim had to go to jail and be shut up, forced to do awful things. Then, as she stared out the window, she spied Angus loping toward a car approaching the driveway. She let out a cry. It was Hank driving Angela's Volvo with a third person in it. "Michael! It's your parents. And I think it's Kim! I can't believe it!" and she flew to the front door, raced down the steps and got to the car just as Kim climbed out and threw his arms around her. "They dropped all the charges!" He picked her up and twirled her around, then hugged Michael who had been at her side as she greeted Kim. "Unbelievable!" she cried.

"Yes, unbelievable!" Kim said.

Michael was grinning. "I told you there were too many of you. They didn't have room!"

Kim shot him a sharp look. "You mean there's safety in numbers?"

Michael shrugged. "Some times, Kim. The luck of the draw."

Chapter Eleven

Berkeley, May, 1969; Kim was driving his VW bug, and he'd just switched on the radio. KSAN was playing Country Joe and the Fish's I feel like I'm fiixin' to die. Kim turned up the volume. When the band belted out the chorus, "One, two, three, what are we fighting for? Don't ask me, I don't give a damn, Next stop is Vi-et-nam!" He and Gina sang along. Gina was sitting next to him, Michael was in back, and they were on their way to the Memorial Day march. When the band played the last chorus all three yelled out the refrain, Kim whooping with laughter. He caught Michael's eye in the rear-view mirror. Michael had been belting it out, too. Gloomy Michael. Now he was smiling. He figured Michael didn't like the Vietnam war any more than he did.

Kim switched off the radio. They were approaching the campus. "Hey," he shouted, "no Guards, no Blue Meanies. The barriers are down." He turned onto Bancroft and headed for the campus parking lot. He shot a quick glance at Gina. She was staring out the window, tense, watchful. "It looks like they really mean it." she said, quietly, "the campus is open again."

"Maybe we'll have some peace and quiet here for a change," Michael said, eying Kim in the rear-view mirror.

Kim held his gaze. "Michael, maybe we don't want peace and quiet here. The protests must continue. We just want to get rid of the pigs."

Michael didn't respond. When they left the VW and began the walk up the slope to the stadium where the big football games were played, and where they were to gather for the march, they were caught in a stream of fellow marchers. Kim recognized some of the younger ones, but many others walking up the hill were the age of his parents or older. When they entered the stadium he was stunned to see the huge numbers gathered there. Hundreds, maybe thousands! He scanned the bleachers for police or National Guards. He could only see men in Berkeley police uniforms stationed at the exits and at the upper rim of the stadium, but no Guards. He also noted that there were several men and women handing out daisies to anyone who would accept them. Gina, whose hand he held, let go to reach for a handful of the yellow flowers. She smiled. "The Quakers. I heard they were going to do this. What a cool idea."

At one end of the football field a dozen or so well-dressed people, local citizens, maybe, had mounted a platform. A man in a suit and tie spoke into a microphone. Kim found it difficult to hear what he said, but from the movement of the crowd, realized the man was giving instructions to begin the march. In front of the platform a column of men and women were holding up a green banner, but it was too far away to read. Kim watched as the column moved out the exit and the crowd slowly, quietly fell in behind. He glanced at Michael, then Gina, and the three linked arms. Michael on one side of Gina, he on the other, Gina clutching her daisies.

They moved like a swarm of bees, adjusting to the hundreds of bodies pressing around them as they went through the stadium exit and then spread out across the street that had been chosen for the march. Kim, Gina and Michael took their place in a column of quietly chatting marchers, still linking arms. Suddenly, Kim was startled to hear the noise of an airplane engine overhead. He felt Gina flinch, pulling his arm close to her soft breast with her elbow, and they all eyed the sky. "It's just a little airplane," Gina called out, "not a helicopter, and look it's pulling a banner. What does it say?"

Michael, who had turned his head as the airplane moved, said, "let a thousand parks bloom!" The marchers around them whooped with pleasure as they spelled out the words on the banner. The plane flew in a circle over their heads and then disappeared over the bay.

When they reached the park site, Kim could feel Gina's tension again. She slowed her pace, dragging on his arm, her body stiff. He exchanged glances with Michael, who gestured with his free hand at the Guards lined up before the chain link fence edging the park area. The marchers spread out along the streets surrounding the park and stopped. From a block or so away he could hear a band playing a Beatles song. The platform holding the march organizers was around the corner from where they were standing.

As they came to a halt, Kim was startled to see three of the girls who had walked in the column just ahead of them, dance forward to the motionless Guards. The men stood shoulder to shoulder holding their rifles across their chests. The girls were smiling as they drew closer and then stood on their tiptoes to place a daisy into the barrel of the Guard's rifle. Kim held his breath. The Guards didn't move—except one blue-eyed young soldier whose mouth twitched at the corners in a repressed smile. At that moment Gina wriggled free from his and Michael's arms, and with a daisy held out, approached another Guard and placed her flower. She turned back to Kim and Michael and gave them both triumphant smiles. Kim found himself laughing. What did these girls think they were accomplishing? Daisies! He glanced at Michael, who was smiling at her admiringly. There was something about how Michael looked at Gina he didn't like.

Then from the distance he heard the band stop playing and the sound of a voice on a loudspeaker, but he couldn't understand what was being said. The crowd around them moved restlessly. He noted that several marchers were leaving, heading for the streets away from the park. He exchanged looks with Michael and Gina. "Shall we get out of here? It seems to be over." They nodded, and Michael led the way through the shifting bodies.

When they reached Telegraph Avenue, eying its many boarded-up windows, Gina said she wanted to go toward campus. "I want to see if the Guards and cops have really gone. Maybe someone knows something about finals or graduation schedule—or when the next quarter will start."

"OK," Kim said. "OK Michael?"

"Sure," Michael said, and they continued along the crowded street, Kim thinking about the march, how it had attracted thousands of participants, and had certainly been peaceful. Whether it had been effective it was too soon to say. Would Reagan withdraw the troops? He hadn't yet. The hippie bit with the flowers was stupid, of course. "Hey, Gina, how did you like being a hippie?"

She laughed. "I liked it. Handing out flowers is a hell of a lot better than getting hit on the head, don't you agree Kim?" She gave him a sly glance.

He pondered a moment. "I don't know, Gina," he said, frowning. "But what does it accomplish?"

"Showing friendship, peace, beauty—absence of malice."

Michael slowed his step and fixed his eyes on Gina. "I guess seeing pretty girls handing out flowers makes people feel good for the moment, but the Guards are still there—and the war in Vietnam goes on."

"Right on, Michael!" Kim said, pounding Michael's shoulder. "To hell with handfuls of flowers. Maybe we have to meet violence with violence. Maybe the Panthers have the right idea. They're packing guns. Peaceful marches don't accomplish a fucking thing. If we want change we have to blow those bastards away. Hurt a few. Cut them down."

Michael was staring at him, his eyes as hard as flint, his mouth tightly closed. Gina came to an abrupt halt. "Kim, you're out of your mind! Those Blue Meanies must have wrecked your brain. We want peace not fucking war! Remember?"

After a long pause Michael spoke slowly, firmly. "Come on, Kim. Enough talk of violence. Maybe Gina's right. Something's happened to your brain. And I think I've had enough of Berkeley. For Christ's sake let's stay sane!"

As Michael reached his Ford, he looked up and waved to Gina who was watching him from the upstairs window of her Bancroft co-op. He'd been helping her bring the few belongings she'd had at his parents' house up to her room. That afternoon after the march, when she'd discovered that the campus was no longer occupied by police or Guards, and that Finals would begin June 7, only a week away, she'd decided to pack up and return to her usual residence. He'd also needed to leave, since the following day he was expected back at his part-time job at the Stanford computer center. Gina had asked him for a ride—not Kim. It was obvious that she was not happy about Kim's sudden militant talk.

Now she was waving at him, wishing him luck, smiling warmly, and from her open window, laughing, she tossed a yellow daisy to him, which fell at his feet. He picked it up, held it to his nose, feeling an urge to throw her an Italianate lover's kiss, but resisted. He was feeling a mixture of emotions—pleasure at her presence—and a puzzling regret at parting. When he was with her, she lifted his spirits, caused him to feel more alive. He tore his eyes away from her, climbed into his car, turned on the ignition and waved out the window as he drove off. He had to keep reminding himself that she was Kim's girl. She was off-limits. What would happen to Kim's relationship with her now? Had her feelings for Kim shifted? He glanced at the daisy he'd placed on the dashboard, thinking of Gina and Kim's teasing sarcasm about her being a hippie. And what about Kim? Was he foolish enough to consider joining some pro-violent group like a section of SDS?

As he approached the bridge the traffic was dense. He thought of the horde of people he had been with on the peace march. So many protesters and so well-behaved, almost solemn. It was Memorial Day, of course, and people couldn't stop from considering the plight of the young Americans fighting in the Vietnam jungles. In their mind's eye they'd all be re-playing the news footage they'd watched on television, the steaming tropical jungle, the helicopters retrieving soldiers, either alive or dead, the napalmed Vietnamese children. Some of them may have sons fighting there. And they couldn't help but feel anger and resentment toward Governor Reagan's militancy, his occupation of their city, the killing of one of their citizens and the blinding of another. And the National Guards were still bivouacked in the fenced park site. When would they be withdrawn?

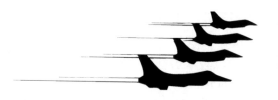

Chapter Twelve

June, 1969, Palo Alto; The next day as Michael performed his tasks at the computer center, he kept replaying his past two weeks in Berkeley. He couldn't get the image of Gina's Botticelli face from his mind. She would be studying for finals at the moment. Kim also. At least he hoped Kim had decided to get back to work, to put aside his radical behavior and consider his future.

Last night he'd called home and Dad had said that Kim was holed up in his room surrounded by books and papers and drafting tools. Dad had sounded troubled, particularly about the possibility that the FBI would receive a report of Kim's arrest and could now be included in their files of possible subversives. Dad had been thinking about his own FBI or NSA file, of course, and the top secret clearance he needed at the Laurence lab.

Michael wondered if he, too, should be concerned about his brother's questionable record? As a physicist he'd most likely need a security clearance—possibly even as a grad student—depending on how Stanford's policies concerning classified research would proceed. The divestiture of S.R.I. from Stanford was still up in the air. It wasn't certain how the Physics and Engineering professors would deal with the change. That morning he'd checked with the department, and his status as a prospective grad student was in order, at least. He'd also received information about his Commencement, which was scheduled for Sunday the week after next. Dad had said he and Mom would come—and maybe Kim. Would Kim bring Gina? She'd said she'd never been to Stanford and wanted to visit. It would be fun to show her around—and Kim, of course, although he'd been here several times.

Now, at the end of his shift, he biked across campus to his house near Stanford Ave. Only two of his housemates were here during the break—Julie and Ron. Alistair had gone home to Philadelphia for the summer. Ron had a job at Hewlett-Packard—in the mail room. Julie was immersed in her radical activities, but he hadn't yet found time to talk to her about them.

Neither Julie nor Ron had been at home when he arrived from Berkeley the evening before. He'd been loaded with groceries he'd stocked up on at the Palo Alto Co-op on California Ave and was trying to find space for them when Julie rushed in. Shouting a surprised "hey stranger!" hoop earrings glinting, flowered cotton shift fluttering, she disappeared into her room. Within seconds she rushed out again carrying a stack of pink fliers. She handed him a sheet, called out a "bye Michael," and sped out the door.

Startled, he stood a moment, the pink sheet in his hand and stared at the door Julie had disappeared through. Then he glanced at the flier. In large letters at the top of the paper was the name Revolutionary Union. Below was an announcement about an orientation meeting, where and when it would be held. The Revolutionary Union, it said, was a Maoist organization dedicated to revolution, dictatorship of the proletariat, democratic centralism and armed struggle. All were welcome. At the bottom of the page was the line The people and the people alone are the motive force in the making of world history. Mao Tse Tung.

He'd continued to stare at the pink piece of paper in his hand, not wanting to believe what he was reading. Julie wasn't just an anti-war radical, she now was a Maoist revolutionary. He'd found himself laughing. What next! He'd tossed the flier into the waste basket and finished putting away his groceries.

Now, as he put his bike away in the garage, he thought about Julie and her radicalism, wondering how her navy commander father would react if he knew she was now a Maoist. He smiled to himself. But it wasn't funny, really. It spelled more trouble. He'd had enough trouble the last few weeks. He went into the house and glancing around, concluded neither of his roommates were home.

After going through the mail he'd picked up from the mailbox, he went into the kitchen, took a TV dinner out of the freezer, put it in the oven and grabbed a beer from the fridge. He hadn't been hungry enough to eat out. Popping off the cap he sat at the kitchen table and waited for his whatever-it-was to heat up. It felt strange, somehow, to be back at Stanford without classes to attend. No excitement. No sit-ins. Then he thought of Julie and gave a wry laugh. It wouldn't be long! Her radical friends would cook up some excitement, for sure.

Just as he was setting his very hot TV dinner onto the table, he heard a car pull up in the driveway and then girls' voices, one of them Julie's. The door burst open and two chattering blondes flitted in. Julie tossed Michael a beaming smile. "Michael, you're really back. We've missed you." She then turned to the second girl, a slender, pretty, blue-eyed blonde with shining hair hanging to her waist. "This is Tracy, Tracy Collins. She's in my RU group. Michael Bardot, my roommate."

Tracy smiled, and they exchanged greetings, Michael puzzling over what Julie's RU group could be. Then his glance lit upon the waste basket. He remembered the pink flier. Of course, RU, the Revolutionary Union. His eyebrows were raising. Good God, he thought. This girl Tracy looked like a Barbie doll. What sort of revolutionary could she be? Her short cotton shift was made from an Indian bedspread and was transparent enough for him to see she was bra-less. Her legs were long and shapely and her feet fit neatly into strappy sandals.

Julie proceeded to put on the kettle and reach into the cupboard for something wrapped in foil. Tracy hung her Mexican bag by its strap over the back of the chair opposite him and sat down. As Julie set the foil-wrapped package on a plate in front of Tracy, she glanced at Michael. "So, Michael, tell us about Berkeley. And how's your brother, the one who got beaten by the pigs?"

"He's OK. He had to stay quiet for a few days, but he's good."
He watched Julie as she cut into what he recognized as a carrot cake.

She scooped a piece onto a plate and handed it to him. "Here, have some carrot cake. But tell me, Michael, were you there when that bastard Reagan brought in the National Guards? I saw it on TV."

"No," he said quickly, not wanting to pursue the subject.

Tracy's wide blue eyes were gazing at him. "Yeah, and the Blue Meanies. We should destroy them all." She took a bite of her carrot cake and continued. "Our leader at RU said yesterday that we should kill the pigs and the pig babies, too. Cut them down."

Michael choked on a mouthful of cake. He stared at her. The girl was smiling. She showed absolutely no emotion. She might have been telling him how to peel apples. He blotted his mouth with his napkin and sat back in his chair, wondering what she'd say next.

"Right on!" Julie said, cutting into the cake, serving herself. "And he said we should create police confrontations, discredit the pigs, scream out 'Police Brutality!!'" The kettle whistled and she rose to make the tea. "Bruce says all the revolutionary groups should cooperate—the Panthers, the Red Guard, Venceremos, and begin the armed revolution in three years."

Michael watched Julie as she made the tea and poured out three cups. Armed revolution? The more he heard the greater was his alarm. "Is this group leader, Bruce, Professor Bruce Franklin?" he said, finally, casually, "the Stanford English professor?"

"Yeah", Tracy said, reaching for her cup. "Sometimes we have meetings at his house. His wife is real nice. I told him that I was letting some of our members keep their stash of weapons in my house in Menlo Park and he was quite interested."

Michael stared at her. Had he heard correctly? "Tracy, you store guns in your house? Does your landlord know?"

Her blue eyes widened. "It's my house, Michael. My grandmother left it to me in her will. Along with the trust fund. I can do what I want there. And the guns are for self defense if the pigs attack. And we have permits for them. Professor Franklin said that if we had permits nobody could object."

Julie then spoke up. "And he said it was good for us to learn how to shoot to defend ourselves."

"And are you both in Professor Franklin's class?"

Julie nodded. "I am, not Tracy."

"Oh no," Tracy said. "I'm not a student here. I went to college in Austin. Now I'm taking classes at Foothill Community College—in practical nursing—so I'll be ready."

"Oh," was all he could think to say. He'd heard enough. His head was swimming. He rose and put his empty TV dinner tray in the garbage can under the sink. "Well, I'll be going up to my room. Have a good evening, you two!" He raced up the stairs and fled into his sanctuary. Berkeley had been turbulent, but here he was dealing with absolute insanity. Surely this talk of armed revolution and stashed weapons was subversive, maybe illegal. He'd heard of Professor Bruce Franklin. He was an Associate Professor in the English department. HUAC, the House Un-American Affairs Committee would make mincemeat of all of them, Julie and Tracy, too. The FBI were probably already on to them. An agent may be lurking outside at this very moment. What should he do? He should move out of here. Find a new place to live—one without whacky roommates! Maoists, for Christ sake!

Chapter Thirteen

Berkeley, June,1969; Exhausted, Kim shoved open the classroom door and fled down the corridor into the open air. He ran down the building's steps and at the bottom stopped to light a cigarette, wishing it were grass. His fucking finals were over, thank God, but this last one for structural engineering had been a nightmare. He'd been able to answer two of the three problems without going crazy, but the last one was a bitch. Hopefully, he'd passed, which would be a miracle considering what he'd been through the last month. He glanced back at the concrete building, not wanting to think about how to calculate the amount of steel needed to support the material's weight.

He laughed to himself and hurried along the path to Sproul Plaza. Did he truly want to become an architect? During the last few months he'd hardly thought about his prospective career. It had seemed as though his motive for remaining at the University was to avoid being drafted. And it was true, considering the future, a job, a regular life seemed out of the question while the war in Vietnam raged. He'd thought he wanted to make a difference, build beautiful, functional, graceful buildings for everyone, including the poor, but instead he knew that his government was destroying buildings and the people in them in a third world nation. He touched his scalp where he had been beaten by the cop. That blow had changed him, given him a reality check, which had been reinforced by the treatment he had received at Santa Rita. Those victors, government leaders included, preached justice but delivered punishment—the night-stick, the bombs, the napalm. So, what would he do? He wanted to take off, get out of Berkeley, stop the war, bring about change. Instead, he was powerless, trapped.

By now he'd reached Telegraph and Bancroft and only a few students were about. Finals week was almost over. It was late afternoon, and only a few political placards were to be seen. His eyes alighted on the SDS poster which announced the date and place of the national convention to be held in Chicago this summer. He stared at it, suddenly thinking that taking a trip to Chicago could be interesting. He wasn't an SDS member, but he'd been considering joining. They'd done good work at SF State. They were well organized and believed in meticulous planning. Then he thought of Gina. How great it would be if she would go to Chicago with him. He hadn't seen her since the Memorial March. They'd both been studying night and day to catch up with their work. She'd been angry with him, hadn't approved of his militant talk. He glanced down Bancroft toward her co-op, but then turned on his heel and headed for his car. At the moment all he wanted to do was sleep. When he drove into the driveway of his parents' house, he looked at it with displeasure. What was he doing still living at home? He really must get out of here.

That night he crashed. He didn't wake up until daylight, which he knew was a Saturday. He lay in bed for a while luxuriating in the knowledge that the semester was over, that he had no more papers to write or exams to take, and he didn't have a job to go to. That thought caused him to jump out of bed. He needed money if he really wanted to go to Chicago, and that's what he'd been planning when he fell asleep the night before. And he was hungry. After his shower he rummaged around his tiny kitchen for something to eat, but his small fridge was empty except for a moldy chunk of salami. Should he cadge something to eat from his mother? He laughed. There were advantages to living at home after all.

Angela was next to the stove cracking eggs in a bowl when Kim ambled into the kitchen and peered over her shoulder. "Looks good, Mom. Can you add an egg for me? I'm starved."

She turned and gave him a scrutinizing look. She hadn't seen him for days. His beard had grown and instead of his afro-type curls, his hair was almost to his shoulders. She noted the blue shadows under his eyes. "So, Kim, how are you? And your finals? Did you do OK?"

He nodded. "I think so, but you never know. And I'm OK—kind of wiped out, but I'm alive."

After beating the eggs with a fork, Angela poured the mixture into the pan and began to scramble them. "So how's your head? Any problem with the wound?" She glanced up at him and then at Hank, who had just walked into the kitchen, the morning paper under his arm.

"Well, hello stranger," Hank said, placing the newspaper on the table then pouring himself coffee. "Are you still alive?"

"Yeah, Dad, sort of."

"OK, you two," Angela said, scooping eggs onto three plates. "Sit down. Let's have breakfast." She eyed the Chronicles' headlines as she distributed the eggs. Bad news, of course. Vietnam. Over 200 American casualties. She'd seen the latest Life magazine, the one with the cover showing one of the soldiers killed. Inside were photographs of all of these young men. She folded the paper over so that the headlines were not visible. She wanted to avoid hearing Hank and Kim get into yet another Vietnam dispute. When that subject was aired it always ended with anger. One or the other would march out of the room fuming. "So, Kim, this quarter is actually over. Do you know what you'll be taking next?"

"Yeah, I guess so." His tone indicated he had no intention of elaborating. He frowned, spread out the newspaper and stared at the headlines. Angela watched as his expression hardened. He looked up from the newspaper and then at Hank. "I've been locked up in my room studying this last week. Do you know anything about this?" and he held up the paper so that Hank could read the headline. In large black letters it said, 247 American Soldiers Killed Last Week.

Hank set down his fork. "I know only that it was a disaster."

Kim's eyes were blazing. He jumped up from the table. "You people don't care! You don't care that during last week 247 American young men were slaughtered because a bunch of men in the White House and the Pentagon have to show how powerful they are. They're scared shitless they'll lose their jobs, have their property stripped from them."

Angela stood up and touched Kim's arm. "Of course we care, Kim. You know Hank and I are against this war. The government got caught up in it and nobody seems to know how to get out of it."

"No, instead we go in deeper, bomb Cambodian supply lines, bomb north Vietnam villages, slaughter our own young men."

Hank was staring at Kim. "So, Kim, what do we do? We had an election and the majority of Americans voted for Nixon. His platform was clear. He would fight Communism. He would continue the Cold War and the war in Vietnam. Americans are afraid of Russia. They're terrified of nuclear war. They voted for him."

"So now we have to wait for another four years to get rid of him? How many more Americans have to die? There has to be another way. Maybe democracy doesn't work!" and he slammed down the newspaper and moved toward the door.

Hank answered slowly. "It works most of the time, Kim."

Kim's eyes still blazing, he stared at Hank. "Well, it's not working now. And speaking of nuclear war, do I need to remind you of the work you do?"

Hank took a deep breath but before he could answer, Kim stormed out of the house. Angela could hear his car skid on the gravel as it backed out of the driveway. Her heart clenched.

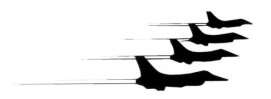

Chapter Fourteen

June,1969, Palo Alto; Sunlight dappled the sidewalk and the morning air was fresh as Michael pedaled back to his house off Stanford Ave. He was feeling pleased about the room on campus he'd just agreed to rent. It was over the garage of one of his former Professor's house and had it's own bathroom and kitchen alcove and he'd be able to move in the first of July. He would also start his new job at SRI in July, full time during the summer, part time when classes began, so he was all set. It would be a tremendous relief to be away from Julie and her crazy friends. He continued to experience jolts of shock at their Maoist talk. Somehow, the wide blue eyes and shimmering blonde hair didn't match the militant rhetoric. He agreed with them when they spoke in horror of the bombing of the villages and towns in North Vietnam, but from what he'd read about Mao and his revolution he was revolted by Julie's rants praising him.

Yes, it would be a great relief to get those idiots out of his hair. He was also looking forward to the next day, his graduation. His parents were coming and he'd been able to track down Kim, who promised to bring Gina. Kim was in a rebellious mood at the moment, unfortunately. Mom had told him that Kim had slammed out of the house after a fight with Dad again. She hadn't seen much of him, but she'd called that morning to say that he'd agreed to go to his graduation, but he'd take his own car.

The following day Michael found himself in a flurry of preparations for both the ceremony that afternoon and the celebration afterwords. His parents had arranged to take him, Kim, Gina and his housemate to dinner at Jack's in San Francisco after the ceremony, and Julie was organizing a party here at the house after the dinner. Michael knew she'd found a good supply of Acapulco gold and plenty of beer. He just hope nobody would drop acid. At the last party he'd attended one of the guys, believing he could fly, dived out a window and broke his leg. Michael had discouraged his parents from attending the party. It most certainly wasn't their scene. Kim and Gina would stay, he supposed. As he tied his tie, peering into the mirror, he found himself grinning. He wondered if that bimbo, Tracy, would come to the party. What would Kim think of her? Julie was attending the commencement ceremony. Ron, too.

The afternoon proceeded as expected. The sun shone, the graduates looked sharp, clean, in their caps and gowns. The professors were regal in their varied robes and hoods and the speeches no more boring than usual. In fact, the student valedictorian spoke eloquently, touching on the events of the past few months, the protests, the agreement to remove classified research from campus. The students in the audience gave the valedictorian a standing ovation. Many of the parents remained seated.

The dinner with his parents went well enough. They both were obviously pleased with him and were charming to Julie and Ron. Kim seemed to have dropped his rebellious, militant talk. He and Dad were polite to each other and Kim immediately hit it off with the Stanford housemates. Michael noted gratefully that they avoided potentially inflammatory subjects that could offend the parents and thereby spoil his party. He watched Kim for a moment, fondly remembering the good times they used to have together backpacking in the Sierra. Now Kim was exchanging anecdotes with Ron about concerts they had attended at places like the Fillmore. What was going on in Kim's head these days? Michael eyed Gina, who sat between the two. She would know. She was cutting into her rack of lamb, glancing from one to the other, listening but not participating. Like Michael, himself, she remained quiet. He noted how her eyes flickered in the candlelight as she turned from one to the other of the young men. Then her glance met his for a fleeting moment before she looked away. Had he been staring?

When the dinner was over Hank and Angela left for Berkeley, first presenting Michael with a handsome $1,000 check. Michael then rode with Julie and Ron back to his house and Kim drove Gina. Michael was disappointed he hadn't yet had a chance to talk to Gina alone. As he gazed out the car window at the flashing lights along the freeway, he decided try to corner Gina at the party. She would be able to tell him was happening to Kim.

When they arrived at the house some of their friends were already there. Julie had assigned some of her SDS and Revolutionary Union comrades to set out the food and drinks and to hook up the music system. When Michael walked in the door he was confronted with the blare of what he recognized as a Jefferson Airplane piece. He worried about the neighbors, but figured they must be used to the clamor. It was Commencement day, after all and students were expected to celebrate noisily. He lingered at the door and watched the gyrations of the dancers in the middle of the room. The living room rug had been rolled up and the furniture pushed back—and the decibels mounted.

Kim and Gina had followed him inside and he introduced them to the guys he knew from his physics classes and the computer center. There weren't many girls from his own circle of friends. Subjects like physics and computation were almost exclusively a male domain. Fortunately, Julie and Ron had supplied the party with a clutch of pretty women, many of them dancing. Then as he peered around the smoky, noise-filled rooms, it was with a certain amount of trepidation that he spied Tracy in the kitchen. She was deep in conversation with a guy in tattered, dirty jeans, a braid down his back and an unkempt beard. She was dressed in a Mexican embroidered shift. It was so short it barely covered her shapely ass. The guy was probably another Maoist.

As he surveyed the scene, he saw Kim taking a drag on a joint Julie had just handed him. She then took his arm and introduced him to Tracy and her companion. Michael groaned inwardly, searched the crowd for Gina and wound his way toward her. As he approached, she threw him a warm smile. He could feel its heat and his breathing quickened. "Gina," he said, touching her arm, claiming space in the crowded room. He leaned toward her, so she could hear. "It's so great you're here! I didn't get a chance to talk to you at the dinner, but I've been thinking about you, worrying really. Did your finals go OK?"

She nodded, and raising her voice said, "Yeah, I think so Grades haven't come yet. But at least they're over."

"And you're still alive?" he shouted.

"More or less. And what about you, Michael? The trouble with your grad program?"

"It seems to be working out. . ." He stopped in mid-sentence, the music was so loud it was really impossible to talk. "Gina, let's go outside. It's warm enough. It's too damned noisy in here." He held her arm and guided her to the French doors that led into the small garden patio where a handful of Julie's guests were quietly smoking and talking. Michael led Gina to a bench on one side of the patio. "Here. Let's sit for a while. Maybe now we can talk."

The patio was dimly lit and although he could hear the pounding of a Grateful Dead tune from inside, he didn't need to shout, and the air was pleasant. He could smell the jasmine that climbed the fence behind them. He watched as Gina smoothed her short blue skirt and settled back against the wooden bench, then suddenly remembering his manners said, "but can I get you something? Something to drink or eat. . .or smoke? Julie set out lots of good stuff."

Gina shook her head. "No, really, Michael. After all that food and wine at Jack's, I'm good." She turned to him, and hesitating, gave him a puzzled look. "Michael, I've been wondering. . .are you and Julie. . . well, are you two dating?"

He laughed. "No, for Christ's sake, no! She's Alistair's girl, our other housemate, but he went home to Philadelphia as soon as classes were over. Julie's a revolutionary. She and Tracy." He shifted on the bench and lowered his voice. "In fact, I'm going to move out of this place. I've rented a room on campus in a Professor's house—over the garage. Julie's a generous girl, but her talk of Mao and armed revolution is just too much! He took a deep breath, aware of the scent of jasmine, and then said abruptly, "no I'm not dating anyone right now. There was someone, but we broke up. About a year ago." He didn't want to remember that painful breakup and shoved the memory away.

"Oh," was Gina's only response.

He stretched his arm behind her and rested it on the back of the bench. His fingers wanted to lift a strand of her silky hair just an inch or so away. His glance fell on the graceful arch of her neck. Then he thought of Kim and shifted his arm to his side. They were both quiet for an endless moment. "So how is my little brother behaving since the park fiasco?" he said, finally.

She looked startled, but answered him quickly. "Actually, he's behaving oddly. He wants me to go with him to Chicago."

"Chicago! What the hell?"

"Yeah. To the SDS convention next week. He's not even a member, but he's thinking of joining. He says he likes what they did at SF State. They cooperated with the Black Power and the Third World people and won what they went on strike for."

"So will you go with him?" He held his breath waiting for her answer, hoping she'd refused.

She shook her head, and pushed a lock of her hair behind her ear. "No, I really hate his new radicalism. At first I thought it was just talk, but I think he's changed. I haven't told him yet, but I won't go to Chicago with him. My family needs me at home, anyway."

As she spoke, Michael realized that Kim and Julie were ambling toward them. "Well, speak of the devil! Hi Kim, Julie." and he stood up to greet them. "It's a great party, Julie. Thanks for all the work."

Julie was beaming. "Yes, it is a good party, but we came out here to ask you, Michael, if you'll go with us to Chicago next week."

He laughed. "Me? Chicago! Gina was just telling me. . .the SDS convention. No thanks. That's just not my scene." He glanced at Kim, who looked a little stoned. "So how will you get there, and where will you stay?"

Kim grinned. "You mean where will I get the bread? We figure we won't need much. Ron and Tracy will come, too. We'll take Julie's Ford and share the cost of gas, take turns driving—camp, maybe, along the way. And Julie says her friend Alistair will meet us in Chicago. He has friends who belong to a commune where we can crash. Cool, huh?"

Michael stared at him. "Yeah, cool." He watched as Kim took his place on the bench next to Gina. Julie then took hold of Michael's arm and dragged him toward the house. "Come on, graduate. Tracy has been asking for you. Your guests await!"

He shot another glance at Gina, whose eyes held his for an instant, then allowed himself to be led away.

The day after Michael's graduation Hank and Angela were relaxing on their sunny deck in Berkeley after breakfast. The fog lingered in drifts over San Francisco, but it was pleasantly warm. Angus dozed in the sunshine, sprawled on the warm redwood planking, his black nose resting on his paws. Angela idly sipped her coffee, and Hank was stretched out on the deck chair. He was reflecting upon the new project at his lab, remembering Kim's cutting taunt about the work he did on nuclear weapons. He must tell Kim about the bio-medical research he and the newly-hired molecular biologist were planning. They'd received the OK to go ahead with the new division only last week. He would no longer be working on nuclear weapons, thank God, and the new project would not be top secret. He hadn't talked about it yet because the program was still in the infant stage and he hadn't been sure if it would be approved by the Atomic Energy Commission.

He now glanced at the Sunday Chronicle on the table in front of him, relieved to think that now he wouldn't have to feel guilty about his own involvement when he read about possible threats of nuclear war. When he opened the paper the headline on the front page caught his eye. After reading the article, datelined Midway Island, he glanced up at Angela, who seemed to be lost in thought as she gazed out at the bay. He lowered the newspaper, and tapping the page, said, "Angela, it's hard to believe, but Nixon says he's going to withdraw 25,000 troops from Vietnam!"

Startled, she stared at him, the coffee cup in hand, motionless, "my God, Hank, has something happened?"

"Nixon's meeting with Thieu, the South Vietnamese President and Thieu says the Vietnamese soldiers will be taking over fighting the Vietcong from the Americans. They call it Vietnamization. Nixon also says peace talks are going ahead in Paris. We need to be patient, he says. Give him three months."

Angela straightened her back and stared at him. "But I read yesterday that savage bombing continues on Hanoi and other population centers. Nixon may talk about peace, but our airmen are slaughtering people. He asks for patience? And we're losing two hundred of our own boys every week?"

Hank sighed, dropping the paper on the table, thinking of their own sons. The dinner with them last night had been pleasant. They'd managed to avoid the troublesome subject of Vietnam. He and Kim had been a little awkward with each other, remembering the harsh words spoken the day before, but they'd been polite. And Michael seemed happy, relieved to have settled his grad program—and finding a new small apartment of his own. He turned to Angela, who had picked up the paper and was now reading it "So, Angela, what did you think of Michael's housemates?"

She lowered the paper and after reflecting a moment said, "they seem good enough kids. Julie writes poetry, she told me. And Ron will start rehearsal in As you Like it in July."

Hank nodded. "Interesting. And everyone avoided talking politics, protests and the war."

She laughed. That they did! They've all been well brought-up. They wouldn't want to spoil Michael's special day. Julie told me her father is a commander in the navy, stationed in San Diego. Ron's Dad is in the production department at MGM. Lives in Beverly Hills. They've been taught how to behave when they need to."

Hank gazed out at the bay, reflecting on Angela's words. "Well, Stanford students are more conservative than those at UC Berkeley. They come from richer families."

She tossed him a sly glance. "You mean like Michael?"

He shrugged. "Well—not all Stanford students are rich, of course. I meant generally, but Michael is certainly more conservative than Kim, I'll say that."

"He's always been more cautious, more contemplative, the observer. Kim's the activist—has always jumped into the fray with both feet."

From the back steps, Hank then heard Kim's voice. "Am I hearing my name?" and he hopped up the last step onto the deck. He laughed. "So, you guys enjoying the sunshine?"

Hank gave a tentative smile, noting Kim's vibrancy, which was strange considering he'd been to the party at Michael's last night. Normally after partying the night before Kim moved as if he were half dead. "Indeed, Kim, it's a lovely day. So how was the party?"

"Great!" He leaned back on the deck railing, still smiling. Angus came prancing toward Kim. Kim patted his head and murmured a greeting.

Angela lifted her coffee cup. "Coffee's on the stove, Kim."

He shook his head. "Thanks, but I don't have time. . I just wanted to tell you. . ." He stopped in mid sentence and pushed himself up on the railing, obviously searching for a way to tell them something they might not want to hear. Hank focused on Kim's face, wondering what he would shock them with this time.

Kim finally continued. "I want to tell you that tomorrow morning I'll be on my way to Chicago with Julie and Ron. You met them last night."

Hank and Angela said in unison "Chicago?"

"Yeah, to the SDS convention. Everyone will be there."

Angela sat up straight in her chair. "But, Kim, you told me you didn't join SDS."

"I know, but now I'm going to join. Mom, y'know, it was you who told me they organized the strike at State really well. They've been effective—also at Stanford. Julie and Ron took part in the sit-ins at Stanford. They're both SDS."

Hank felt his anger mount. Did Kim expect him to finance this trip? What had got into him? What did he think he would accomplish? He glanced at Angela, whose lips were tightly closed as she eyed him, telling him mutely to calm down. He breathed in the fresh air. "So, Kim, a trip to Chicago could be expensive. Can you afford it?"

"I think so, Dad. I've got a couple of hundred dollars and it shouldn't cost much. We'll drive in Julie's Ford. And camp along the way—and share the cost of gas. And Julie has a friend in Chicago where we can all stay."

Hank shot a glance at Angela, who looked stricken. "Kim," she said, "Promise me you'll be careful. Please, don't take any chances. You saw on TV what the Chicago police and the guards did to the demonstrators at the Democratic Convention last year. Your brain doesn't need another blow on the head!"

"Your mother's right, Kim. For Christ's sake be careful!"

Kim gave him an impatient look and hopped down from the railing. "I'll be careful, don't worry. But now I'm off. I've packed my stuff and I'm going over to Stanford. We're leaving tonight after we've packed Julie's car. Maybe Michael will wave us off. See you after I get back!" and he kissed Angela on the cheek and waved to Hank. Motionless, Hank watched as Kim trotted down the steps and disappeared. He listened as Kim started his car and backed it down the graveled driveway.

Chapter Fifteen

C hicago, June, 1969; Kim rode shotgun next to Ron, who was at the wheel of Julie's Ford. Since Ron was the only one of the four Californians who had spent time in Chicago, the others had insisted he pilot them through the traffic. They were on North Lakeshore Drive, and according to the map in Kim's hand, they were approaching the neighborhood surrounding Northwestern's Chicago campus. Alistair had given them directions to his friend's apartment building, and Kim was the navigator. "At the next exit we should turn on Michigan Ave and follow the directions to the hospital." Kim said, watching for street signs. "The med school is there, Alistair says, and the law school just beyond." Kim had been told that Alistair's friend was a first year law student, and had gone to prep school with him at Andover, and that Alistair, a Poli Sci major also planned to go into law.

After circling the neighborhood several times they finally found the brick building indicated on Alistair's makeshift map, and Ron pulled up to the curb in front of an imposing entryway. From under the blue and white awning a doorman approached, and after Kim explained that they were guests of Mr. James F. Dalton, and after checking his notes, the doorman politely suggested they enter the building. "The valet will park your car and carry up your luggage," he said brusquely. From inside the car Kim could hear Julie and Tracy giggling. Kim had difficulty repressing his own laughter. Besides the girls' two small, scarred suitcases, their luggage consisted of rolled up sleeping bags, dusty army duffels and cardboard boxes filled with camping equipment.

The grimy travelers, canvas bags and purses slung over their shoulders, trudged onto the thick carpets in the elegant lobby. At the desk the concierge scrutinized them with some disdain before he picked up the phone and in icy tones announced their arrival. Then with a peremptory snap of his fingers he called the bellman to "show the visitors to Mr Daltons's apartment seventy-seven on the 7th floor." As he spoke, Kim watched as another man arrived with a cart piled with their bags, duffels and sleeping bags.

Dazed, Kim and his companions followed the red and gray-clad bellman who'd taken control of the luggage cart. So this was the commune Julie had described? He'd expected a drafty loft in the port region or the stockyard. He glanced at Julie and Tracy, both with their dirty, tangled hair, sweat-streaked faces, stained T-shirts and filthy jeans. Ron looked like a derelict from a flophouse. Kim ran his fingers through his own snarled hair. As they waited at the elevator doors, people stared at them with eyebrows raised or smiles twitching at the corners of their mouths.

When they finally reached the door of apartment seventy-seven and it was opened at their knock, they were confronted by a blast of rock and the smell of grass. Beyond the open door Kim scanned the littered room, its empty soda and beer bottles, overflowing ashtrays, stacks of leaflets, scattered bits of clothing, and jeans-clad bodies, both men and women, sprawled on couches, chairs and on the floor. "Hey," one of them shouted, "come on in. Are you the dudes from California?"

Then emerging from a room in the depths of the apartment, two tall guys dressed in clean jeans ambled toward them. With a happy cry, Julie ran to one of them and threw her arms around his neck. It was Alistair, of course, who then introduced Jim Dalton to the California crew. Kim noted the wavy blond hair that fell to Jim's shoulders and the well-muscled shoulders under his green army T shirt. The guy was probably a crack tennis player. Jim was smiling, his gray eyes welcoming. "Hey, you guys, how was your trip?"

Kim flicked the hair back from his eyes. "Long," he mumbled.

"Yeah," Julie said, folding herself into Alistair's encircled arm. "And we need to clean up, like take a shower maybe?"

"Sure," Jim said, "come on, we're kind of crowded. We've got people from all over— Columbia, Yale, Kent State—and now you guys from Stanford and Berkeley, but I'll show you the bathrooms and a room where you can crash, if you want," and he led them through a hallway, pointed to one of the bathrooms and entered one of the several bedrooms that opened onto the corridor. Mattresses were spread over the floor, and the bed and dresser had been pushed back to the wall. "So, make yourselves comfortable. I think there's enough room for you in here."

That evening, after they returned from the nearby coffee shop, Kim and his comrades gathered with Jim and the other SDSers sprawled on chairs and the floor, smoking pot and asking questions about the next day's convention. Julie, who sat on the floor across the room from Jim, the law student, was the first to speak up. "Jim, can you tell us who will be there tomorrow—like other organizations besides SDS?"

Jim tapped the ashes from his cigarette into a glass ashtray. "Well, a bunch from the Progressive Labor party will be there for sure. They're trying to make an alliance with SDS."

"Is that the PL we keep hearing about? Sort of a communist worker's party?"

"Right. Progressive Labor is pro-China Maoist. They broke from the U.S. Soviet-linked Communist party."

Alistair, who was sitting next to Julie, laughed, "Their members are constantly quoting from the little red book."

Jim nodded. "Yeah, at the drop of a hat! What they want is for workers and students to join forces. They've already organized sections of the workers, students alliance, or WSA, within SDS chapters like the one at Harvard."

Kim eyed the room, trying to figure out who the Harvard dudes might be. All this organization shit didn't interest him much.

Jim was still speaking. "And from what I hear PL doesn't think much of the Panthers, maybe because they're not white, although they say it's because they spout incorrect interpretations of Mao's sayings."

Julie exchanged glances with Alistair, then Kim. Jim took a drag on his cigarette. She turned again to Jim. "So who else will be at the convention?"

"Well, you know that SDS welcomes anyone against the Vietnam war and for the rights of blacks, women and the third world. We can expect other left-leaning groups to be there." He grinned, "be they Yippies, Crazies, Panthers, Quakers or Maoists."

Kim had read about the Yippies. They brought street theater wherever they went. Alistair had just shown him a Yippie flier that said all sorts of crazy things—like people should be crazy, freaky, irrational, sexy, and burn draft cards and diplomas and say to hell with your goals. Kim smiled to himself and then at Tracy. The convention would be a trip, for sure, but Jim was still speaking, and he better listen.

"Actually, Jim said, "from what I hear, the national office isn't at all happy about PL taking over some of their chapters. They say there'll be 500 or so uncommitted delegates at the convention. PL hopes to win them over. So the SDS national committee is suggesting something new. SDS would be called the Revolutionary Youth Movement. It would get college students and working class young people to work together. They'd use Dylan's line *you don't need a weatherman to tell you which way the wind blows.* You just have to look around to see what's happening."

Kim found himself touching the scar on his scalp where the policeman had hit him, and remembering Santa Rita. He sure knew what was happening and he wanted to do something about it. Suddenly, he felt turned on. Excited. He was here in Chicago. Maybe now he could make a difference.

Tracy, who was sitting close to Kim called out, "is SDS Maoist?"

Jim hesitated a moment, as if uncertain about his answer. "Some individual SDS members may be Maoists. As I said, SDS welcomes others."

"But the Panthers are Maoists, aren't they?" Tracy said.

Jim laughed. "Right on. And they're everyone's darling at the moment. They've got guns and they don't object to brandishing them at politicians."

Kim remembered reading about the Panthers confronting Governor Reagan in Sacramento, guns in hand, and then again at the S. F. airport. He suppressed a laugh. California allows people to carry guns if they're visible, so the Panthers really make them visible. Far out. Tomorrow's convention should be fantastic.

Early afternoon the next day almost the entire gang made its way by public transportation to the Coliseum on the south side of town. Three of Jim's guests had been too stoned to make it. Julie stayed close to Alistair. Ron had paired off with a Yalie girl, a theater major, and Tracy glued herself to Kim's side. Kim didn't mind, really, but he was surprised to find that she was so dependent on him. She'd sounded so brave and sure when she talked of Mao and revolution. Michael had told him about the guns she allowed Revolutionary Union members to be stashed in her house. He realized he didn't know much about her, except that she had money and came from Texas and she was good to look at. He also guessed she'd be a good lay. He grinned to himself, as holding tightly to her arm, they pressed through the crowd into the Coliseum. The noise was deafening.

Peering around, he noted the crowd was a mix of young and old. There was also a contingent of muscular black men. Otherwise, he couldn't tell who was who. Some of the student-types were high already. On what, he wondered? A man was speaking into a microphone on the platform, but the huge place was so noisy he couldn't hear a word. He and Tracy found seats on one of the bleachers, and Kim scanned the area, searching for their companions who had been swallowed by the swarm of bodies. He felt Tracy's touch on his arm. "I wonder how many people here are undercover cops." she said, "and I saw plenty of pigs in uniform!"

Kim laughed. "Probably equal numbers of pigs and delegates. After the fiasco at the Democratic Convention last year I've been told that Chicago police are out for blood."

That first day at the convention was not at all exciting, Kim concluded. Speakers droned on, people argued, discussions went on endlessly. It was difficult to make sense of it. All the speakers were opposed to the Vietnam war, but spoke about it from different angles. The PL speakers mentioned workers a million times—and Mao Tse Tung. Kim watched delegates wandering in the aisles, gathering in huddles of two or three, and when he went to take a piss he saw them shouting at one another in the corridors surrounding the bleachers. No police action, but lots of talk, discussions, arguments. He also noted the smell of grass and the stoned faces of some of the young delegates. Tracy continued to stick close to him and that evening she unrolled her sleeping bag next to his. He wasn't quite sure what he wanted to do about Tracy, so he grinned to himself, said goodnight and went to sleep.

The next day the Panthers were expected to speak, and most SDS delegates were in their seats waiting expectantly. The Panthers always offered excitement, they said, certainly theater. They had charisma. At least for everyone except the die-hard PL members, who considered them diversionary. Everyone knew about the brandished guns, Huey Newton and the murdered cop. Kim and Tracy were sitting amongst the Stanford contingent. Alistair, a bona fide Stanford delegate, sat on the other side of Kim and filled him in on what he knew about the SDS national leadership and their plans to thwart the PL. "They want to bring the uncommitted delegates along on their plan to shift SDS focus. RYM, it will be called, completely separate from SDS- PL."

Kim forced himself to remember what Jim had told them about RYM, the Revolutionary Youth Movement, supposed to combine university students with working class young people to support the revolution. Kim shrugged. Did all this politicking really matter? They just needed to stop the war, get rid of the pigs, change the world.

Suddenly, Tracy stood up and dragged him to his feet. The crowd around them let out a roar. Four straight-backed black men marched onto the platform. They wore black leather jackets, black pants with black berets perched on their afros. They raised their arms with clenched fist in the Panther salute. The audience exploded with wild enthusiasm, hooting and cheering, the SDS people raising their fists in response. Surveying the crowd Kim noted the delegates who remained seated. He assumed they were PL members.

The convention chairman approached the microphone and the audience quieted. After his introductory words, he said, "and I want to introduce the next speaker. He is the Minister of Information of the Illinois Black Panther Party, Mr. Rufus Walls, best known as Chaka."

Chaka raised his arm and about half the crowd gave him a standing ovation, cheering and whistling. After calming his audience Chaka launched into his speech, vaguely spouting Panther doctrine, slashing at the Progressive Labor party and their misinterpretation of Mao doctrine. He then wandered into the subject of women's liberation. "Yeah, man! We Panthers truly believe in pussy power!"

Kim couldn't believe what he'd heard. It was as if lightening had struck the building sucking the oxygen from the air. For a brief moment they didn't breathe. Then suddenly the cries of "Fight male Chauvinism!" blasted the air. Within seconds the previously quiet PL members took up the chant "Fight Male Chauvinism." Soon, the entire audience was yelling the phrase. Alistair leaned toward Kim and whispered into his ear. "Those PL dudes don't give a fuck about women's rights. It's a diversion, they say, from the path to armed revolution, but listen to the bastards!"

Kim didn't take his eyes off Chaka. He could see that the Panther was visibly confused. He'd turned to his his bodyguards for help but they remained speechless. Finally, Chaka squared his shoulders and reached for the microphone to give it another try, "Y'know, I always figured Superman was a punk because he never tried to fuck Lois Lane." The shouts grew even louder. Chaka stepped away from the podium and another Panther stepped to the microphone. He tried to calm the crowd by spouting the usual Panther doctrinal attack on PL, but nobody was listening, so after a long pause said, "Well, fuck, I personally think pussy power is good for the revolution." He peered from one side of the enormous space to the other, and then grinning, said, "Yeah, like Stokely Carmichael said about the proper position of women in the movement—prone!"

Now the entire crowd was on its feet screaming. Finally, Kim watched as Bernardine Dohrn, the SDS-RYM chairwoman, strode to the microphone. Politely, calmly she said that people should try to curb their chauvinism in the interest of unity of the movement, and then she stepped back. The audience was still on its feet, but had stopped shouting, when Jewel Cook, the third Panther bent to the microphone. "The Progressive Labor party must recant—or be counted as traitors to the revolution."

Immediately the roar began again. "Read Mao! Read Mao," Pl members shouted again and again.

"Power to the people!" the Panthers yelled furiously, "power to the people!"

The cacophony grew even louder when PL then countered with "Power to the Workers!"

Kim was on his feet but his head was pounding. He touched the scar on his scalp. He'd hoped for theater, for excitement, but this was more than he'd bargained for. Then he heard the Panthers yelling "Bullshit, Bullshit!" which to Kim seemed most appropriate. He turned to Tracy, who had taken up all the chants—from *Male Chauvinist! to Read Mao! to Bullshit!*

At that moment, Bernardine Dohrn and Mike Judd marched onto the podium. Dohrn grabbed the microphone and announced that she and her fellow SDS-RYM members would leave the meeting to poll the caucus. She strode off the stage, Mike Rudd at her side, and at least half the audience following her. Alistair and Julie were among them. Kim and Tracy trailed behind.

Stanford, three days later; Alone in the empty house, Michael was about to switch off the downstairs lights before going to bed when he heard a car pull up outside the garage. The sounds of car doors opening and people's voices then brought him to a standstill. Listening quietly, he realized he knew those voices. First was Julie's

California drawl then Kim's clear baritone. He opened the back door and hurried out to greet them, anxious to hear their story. They'd returned sooner than he'd expected. He'd read a little about the convention in the Chronicle, which had said that the SDS had split into two factions, but the report hadn't gone into detail.

Kim was unfolding himself from the driver's seat when Michael reached his side. He stretched his back then held out his arms for a brotherly embrace. Michael clapped Kim's shoulders, then stepped back to scrutinize his face, which was grimy and bearded. His eyes were red with fatigue. "So, when did you leave Chicago?"

"Three days ago," Kim answered, shutting the car door behind him. We camped one night in a state park off the highway, but we've driven straight through since yesterday morning—and we're wasted!"

Michael glanced at Kim's car, parked on the street where he'd left it last week. "You'd better stay here tonight, Kim. You look like shit!"

Julie then staggered out of the car. Her hair hung in lank strands around her face and a blueish stain surrounded her half-closed eyes. "Hi, Michael," she mumbled, "giving him a hug. "Jeez, I'm glad to be back" Ron and Tracy then emerged from the car, slowly straightening their cramped bodies.

Michael watched the dusty, disheveled crew shut the car doors and stagger toward the house. "Can I help you bring in your stuff?"

Kim shook his head. "Leave it 'til tomorrow. Just show me where I can crash."

Julie touched Kim's arm. "Yeah, Kim You can have Alistair's room. Tracy, you can stay with me."

Ron, who was still holding Tracy's arm gave a weary grin. "Yeah, See you in the morning, Trace," and he inched toward the stairway to go up to his room.

Michael watched them as they stumbled toward their rooms. "Can I get you guys something to eat—or drink?"

"Tomorrow," Kim said." Moaning, they traipsed out of the kitchen. Julie headed for the bathroom, announcing that she just had to take a shower or die. Michael locked the back door, turned off the kitchen light and called out a "goodnight everybody! And tomorrow you've got to tell me what happened in Chicago!"

It was almost noon the next day before the travelers assembled at the kitchen table. Michael had stayed home, hoping to get a chance to talk to Kim. He wanted, to find out how Kim had been affected by what had happened in Chicago. He was also curious to hear about Alistair and his friend at Northwestern. He'd made a big pot of coffee and left it warming on the stove and had set out the milk and granola and a stack of cereal bowls and spoons. He figured if they wanted something else they could damned well fix it themselves. After finishing his own bowl of granola he fetched the Chronicle from the front steps and spread it out on the table.

Ron was the first to drift into the kitchen. He'd showered and tidied his beard and put on clean jeans and T shirt. "Hey, Michael, how's it goin' man?"

"Good. And how about you? Survive the trip?"

"I guess so," he said, wandering to the stove, pouring himself some coffee. "But too much driving. I don't know why we had to push so hard. Once you start, somehow it's hard to stop." He pulled up a chair and reached for a bowl and the granola. "I'm starved," he said, pouring milk on the cereal.

Michael watched him lean over his bowl, wolfing up huge mouthfuls. He'd obviously need to wait before he began to ask questions about the convention. He heard water pouring in the downstairs bathroom, and a few minutes later Julie wandered in, toweling her hair. "Hi Michael, Ron—you're up."

Michael grinned. "I've been up for hours."

After making a turban of the towel Julie went to the stove and poured some coffee. "You didn't go to work?"

"No, I don't start my new job for another week."

"Yeah, I forgot. And you're moving out about then, too," she said, sitting and fixing her granola.

"Yeah, I've already started going through my stuff—but Julie, I read about SDS splitting up. Here in the Chronicle," and he tapped at the page on the table. "So which side are you on?"

She sighed. "I don't know. It's a mess. Maybe I'll just drop out—stick with RU. That split-up was like a really bad trip. A turn-off, for sure. And talk, talk talk."

Ron then let his spoon rest a moment. "But what about those assholes, those Illinois Panthers?"

Julie shook her head. "Fuck them! Talk about male chauvinists! What rock did they crawl out from under?"

Michael had read that the Panthers had offended people, but the news report hadn't gone into detail. "So what happened? What did they do or say that was so disruptive?"

Ron and Julie both filled him in on the shocking phrases the Illinois Panthers had used that caused pandemonium at the convention. They then described Bernadine Dohrn leading the walk-out—and the politics of the split-up. To make sense of it all they had to give the same lecture to Michael that Jim Norton had given them the evening they had arrived in Chicago, so Michael was filled in on the Progressive Labor Party, the Workers Student Alliance—and RYM, the Revolutionary Youth Movement.

Julie picked up her cereal bowl and put it in the sink. "And besides the male chauvinist shit, the PL and Panthers were bickering about interpretation of Mao's little red book. They argued about everything—every little detail."

Ron grinned. "But, Julie, what did you think of the Panthers' uniform?"

She arched her eyebrows. "Cool, but all they said was bullshit. They were obscene." Her gaze then shifted from Ron to Michael. "And y'know, I know a couple of Panthers here in East Palo Alto, and they don't wear leather jackets and they don't babble about Mao. They talk about poverty, discrimination, and their brothers who've been drafted and are dying in Vietnam. Important stuff. Not like those assholes in Chicago."

While she was still speaking, Michael realized that Kim had entered the kitchen and was standing in the doorway listening to Julie. "Well, hi Kim., did you sleep OK?"

Kim nodded and headed for the stove to pour himself some coffee. "Yeah, I sure did." Scraping back a chair across from Julie, he gave her a thoughtful look. "And I didn't even dream about that farce we witnessed at the fucking convention. And, Julie, talk about a turn-off, a bad trip, that was it! And I agree, where did they find such stupid Panthers. Those idiots should be tied up and gagged. They're bad for the Movement."

Michael grinned. "So did you join with PL-WSA?"

Kim shook his head. "No fucking way! Too much talk."

"How about SDS-RYM?"

Kim held Michael's gaze. "I'm thinking about it. It depends on what they do. I'm not that turned on by all that Mao Tse Tung doctrine—and the fucking little red book. I just want the war to stop—for Kissinger and Nixon to stop lying, to stop killing and maiming, and to stop American imperialism and discrimination against blacks and people of color."

Michael gave him a long, steady look. "You don't want much, do you?"

Kim returned his look and seemed to be searching for words to reply, but Tracy appeared in the doorway, wet hair dangling around her face, dressed in what Michael recognized as Julie's bathrobe. "Hi guys," she chirped, moving toward Kim. She touched him on the shoulder, gave him a sideways, rather complicit look then sat in the chair next to him.

After a brief glance at Michael, as if still considering his answer Kim shoved back his chair, poured Tracy a cup of coffee and returned to his seat. Tracy reached for the last cereal bowl and spooned out her granola. "So here we are, back in California."

"Right," Ron said, "and I have to go to work tomorrow."

"Yeah," said Tracy, "and I have to go home, see what's happening." She turned to Kim. "You're coming with me, aren't you Kim?"

He nodded, then turned to Michael. "Yeah, Michael, I figured I might crash at Tracy's for a couple of days. I don't start my job with the landscape architect until next week."

Michael stared at him, dumbfounded. Kim was staying with Tracy, the self-described Maoist? He wondered what that implied. Hadn't he just heard Kim mock Mao's little red book? Had Tracy changed her politics since the convention? Or has he underestimated Tracy's charms. And what about Gina? He really needed to talk to Kim before he took off—alone—find out what the hell was going on.

Chapter Sixteen

enlo Park, June, 1969; After loading his car and leaving Michael's, Kim drove Tracy to her house in Menlo Park just north of Palo Alto. He parked his VW bug at the curb in front of a Tudor-style, rambling house set back a good distance from the street complete with green lawn and two tall leafy plane tree. They were in an old section of the town. Tracy, who had been sitting next to him, hopped out of the car and dragged her small suitcase and a sleeping bag from the cramped back seat. Kim pocketed his car keys, grabbed his own canvas duffel, and moved quickly to help her carry her belongings up the brick path to the front door. He watched as she moved quickly along the row of stones bordering the flower bed to the right of the front steps. About a third of the way along the border, first darting glances in all directions around her, she lifted one of the stones, reached under it and lifted a key attached to a leather thong. After unlocking the door she looked around again and returned the key under the stone and carefully set the stone back in its place. Tossing Kim a conspiratorial look, she then hopped up on the steps, turned the doorknob and pushed open the door.

Kim had watched this performance, puzzled by its precision. Tracy was acting like a trained intelligence agent or revolutionary. Following her into the house, which seemed to be empty, he noted the neatly arranged couch and chairs, the television, the rows of books on the oak bookshelves—and the absence of clutter. Tracy then led him to one of the bedrooms down a long hallway and pointing, said, "just dump my stuff there on the bed and I'll show you where you can crash."

He eyed the wide bed, covered in a rose satin duvet. "Tracy," he said, trailing after her, "the house seems empty. Do you live here alone?"

She turned and flashed him a wide smile. "Most of the time, but sometimes people come here to stay a few days if they need to, or to have a meeting."

Meetings? Could this be a so-called safe house like he'd read about in spy stories? "You mean for your RU members?"

"Yeah, and others. Like I told you, Kim, I want them to meet you. You can check each other out. They're careful about who they take into the collective, you know."

"Collective? Is that some of your Revolutionary Union jargon?"

She gave him a sharp look. "It's the word we use for our committee. For security. During the last month or so we've tightened our security, become more professional, so to speak. I don't tell people anymore about the weapons stored here, for instance, like I told Michael. We're in collectives of ten people and we don't need to know what the other collective members are doing, what they're responsible for, or who they are. We meet once a week here."

She'd led him into a bedroom next to hers. He dropped his duffel onto the bed under a window and turned to her. "So does this collective have some specific task—or responsibility?" He remembered Michael telling him Tracy allowed people to store weapons in her house.

"I can't tell you, Kim. Not until you're vetted. We have to be fucking careful about FBI informers, y'know." She giggled, and guided him into the kitchen. "We joke about it, but it's a real. Our collective chairman meets with the other chairmen and he heard one of them talk about how he had good evidence that one of his members was an FBI informant, and he wasn't sure how to handle it."

"So who is your collective chairman?"

"His name is Nick Cole and he's a grad student at Stanford. English department. With Bruce Franklin."

Kim had heard about Franklin, the Maoist English Professor, a Melville scholar. Now Kim watched Tracy fill the kettle with water and measure out some tea into a china teapot decorated with pink roses. She set two tea cups and their saucers on the kitchen table and beckoned for him to sit down. As she lit the stove under the kettle, he noted how her tight jeans and T shirt showed off her shapely body. He kept his gaze on her, watching how she moved, like a dancer, almost feline. And yet with her wide blue eyes and shining hair she could be Barbie herself. But he was coming to the conclusion that she wasn't the airhead he'd thought she was. She seemed to be a bona fide revolutionary who knew which way was up.

So what was he doing here? Was it because he was intrigued by Tracy, that she had a beautiful body and obviously would be willing to sleep with him? Or was it because she puzzled him. Was she a hippie airhead or a smart recruiter, a fucking head hunter for the revolution, intelligent and committed? And did he really want to join this communist organization, with its Maoist methods and jargon? Did he want to be part of an armed revolution? He was angry with his government and how this oh-so-holy democracy wasn't working, but did he really think communism would be any different? Revolutions could breed Stalins and Robespierres. He thought of what Dad had told him about Ho Chi Min, how he wanted to be free from colonial rule. His own beef now was U.S taking over where the French and Brits and Dutch left off—except now we were also fighting communism—both Soviet and Maoist. And there was the draft.

The kettle had boiled and Tracy was pouring the steaming water into the flowered tea pot. Somehow the china tea pot and the delicate porcelain cups and saucers weren't what he thought would be found in a collective's kitchen. Had this been her grandmother's house? "Tracy, you said that your grandmother left you this house in her will. Did she live here?"

Tracy put the lid on the teapot before answering. "No, my mother did—when she was at Stanford Law. My grandmother bought it as an investment and a place for my mother to live. That was before oil was found on the ranch."

He watched her as she shifted the teacups. He knew she came from a wealthy Austin family, but Tracy hadn't talked about her parents. "So your mother's a lawyer?"

She shook her head then poured their tea. "She doesn't practice anymore. She's a state senator."

"Far out!" he said, impressed. "And your father's a doctor."

She gave him a direct look. "Right, fucking bourgeois—both of them."

"But not you!"

"No fucking way. I can't stand the way they live, their attitudes, their small mindedness, their politics, their hypocrisy." She took a sip of her tea. "And what about your parents, Kim."

He grinned. "They're not rich enough to be truly bourgeois. My Dad's a scientist, works for U.C. and my Mom's an artist. But they do expect me to consider my future—which means earning a living, which, I guess, makes them fucking bourgeois."

At that moment the telephone rang. Tracy excused herself and disappeared into the living room where Kim remembered seeing the phone placed neatly on a mahogany table. The tidiness of this house had been a surprise to him. Somehow, Tracy was not the type to keep such a clean, neat house. He smiled to himself. Very bourgeois—or, perhaps, it was working class, now that she championed workers. Then he thought of his parents, whom he admired, really—in spite of their bourgeois qualities They irritated him because they wanted him to be someone he couldn't be at the moment, but he loved them. He hated the work his father had been doing at the lab, but his new projects were no longer war related, thank God. His mother was an artist and produced beautiful things.

And there was Michael. This morning before he'd left Stanford Michael had insisted he take a walk with him. They needed to talk, he'd said, alone. And they had talked. At least Michael had talked, lectured, accused him of being hopelessly naïve. "Don't be an idiot," he'd said. "These radicals don't think straight. They're caught up in the drama, the rhetoric, the excitement of engaging in dangerous acts. Most of them don't know what they're talking about. Do they really know what's happening to the people under Mao? Do they know what a monster Stalin was?"

When Kim had finally drowned out Michael's accusations with his own attacks on Michael's willingness to work on C.I.A contracts or weapons to be used in Vietnam, Michael had changed the subject and brought up the name, Gina. "Did you two break up?" he asked.

He'd tried to explain how he and Gina had strongly opposite views about how to protest the war, but it really wasn't any of Michael's business anyway—and he'd run to the car where Tracy was waiting for him.

And now, Tracy returned, smiling. "Nick will be here soon," she said. "He wants to talk to you." She gave him a direct, sharp look, her blue eyes suddenly no longer like blue sky. "He wants to check you out, like I said. You just have to be as truthful as you can."

Kim held her look. "And I'll find out what this collective is all about. And if I can be useful."

Kim was still sitting at Tracy's kitchen table when he heard the front door open and a male voice calling out her name. Tracy's eyes connected with Kim's before she shoved away her tea cup and stood up. "It must be Nick," she said, giving Kim a meaningful look. "He knows where to find the key to unlock the door." Kim took a quick breath, suddenly nervous. He slowly stood up, and forcing himself to stay cool, followed Tracy into the living room where he saw the man by the front door, his back toward them, turning the dead bolt. Kim noted that his blond hair was combed neatly around his ears, he was clean shaven, and his olive green T shirt was tucked into clean jeans. "Hey Nick," Tracy said, smiling, "it's good to see you—and this is Kim, the guy I told you about, Kim Bardot."

Nick gave Kim a sharp look, moved forward and shook his hand . His handshake was firm and energetic. "Nick Cole, glad to meet you. Tracy tells me you might be interested in working with us." Nick's eyes were a penetrating blue, and his high cheekbones gave his face what Kim thought was an aristocratic appearance.

Kim nodded. "Yes, although I need to know more about what you would expect of me—to see if I could be of any use to you."

"Good. Let's talk a while and find out." He paused, glancing at Tracy, "I think we ought to talk privately, OK Tracy?"

"Sure, I'll leave you two at it. Can I bring you some coffee—or tea?"

"Maybe later. OK?" Tracy nodded and left the room, closing the hall door behind her. Nick sat down in one of the beige upholstered chairs facing the front window. On the wall next to him another tall window faced a good-sized walled patio at the side of the house. Kim sank onto the matching couch opposite Nick, wondering how to begin this two-way interrogation. He was filled with doubt, wondering if he should just leave—go back to Berkeley. Nick settled back in the chair, one foot propped on his knee, eying him. "So, Kim, how shall we begin? Tracy said you're at U.C. Berkeley, an architecture major, and you've been involved in the demonstrations, had your head bashed by the pigs—or was it Reagan's National Guard?"

Kim grinned. "The pigs. And at Santa Rita, the fucking Blue Meanies."

Nick gave him a sympathetic look, his blue eyes flecked with humor. "So that should be a motive for revenge."

"You're damned right." Without thinking, Kim's fingers flew to the scar on his scalp.

"So, Kim, can you tell a little bit about your background—school, family, anything you might think we need to know about you?"

Kim shifted in his chair, took a breath and plunged. He'd gone to Berkeley public schools, he said, was in his Sophomore year at U.C., had been a FSM member, served on the People's Park committee, taken part in the Third World Liberation strike—and the People's Park demonstrations. He described his parents' jobs, his brother's conservatism, and his own anger at the government, it's hypocrisy, its treatment of blacks and people of color—and the war in Vietnam. He then told him about his Dad's experiences with Ho Chi Min, how impressed he'd been with the man, how his team had parachuted into the camp to equip Ho's men to fight the Japanese occupiers.

Nick listened without interruption, but when Kim mentioned Ho Chi Minh, a glint of approval skimmed across his face. He sat up straight, put both feet on the floor and bending forward, gave Kim a sharp, direct look. "Do you know how to shoot, how to handle an M-1 carbine or a 9m handgun?"

Kim shook his head. "No. My Dad didn't allow guns in the house. Said they were dangerous where kids were around. And we never hunted."

A shaft of sunlight from the window beside him lit Nick's eyes, turning them into sharp stones. "If you joined us we'd require that you know how to handle at least four weapons. Besides the M-1 and the handgun, you'd learn to shoot a .45 shotgun and a 30.06 carbine rifle. Would you be OK with that? Would you be willing to use it?"

Kim hesitated before answering. If he trained with those guns, he'd certainly be expected to use them. His breathing quickened. His throat tightened. He stared back at Nick, then made the leap. Once again he forced his voice to be cool. He spoke slowly. "I'd be OK with that. It's time I picked up a gun."

Nick stared at him a moment. "Good," he said finally. "I'll have to talk to my chairman, but you sound to me like you'd fit in." He then shifted forward in the chair, as if to get up, but then stopped himself. "You'd need to attend some of our education sessions, of course. And I must say we usually recruit people who know guns, but you sound like you could soon learn." He stood up and smoothed back his hair.

Kim had been concentrating on the gun aspect of his training and had barely heard the words education sessions. He gave Nick a questioning look. "Nick, I'm wondering where the hell do you practice shooting around here?"

"That's something you don't need to know yet. I'll tell you if the collective thinks you're ready. I'll talk to the others and let you know as soon as it's decided. Will you be staying here—or going back to Berkeley?"

"I'll be here tonight, at least. I'm not expected back in Berkeley until next Monday."

"OK," and he shook Kim's hand, and calling out to Tracy, shouted a goodbye. At the door he turned the knob on the dead bolt, and before closing the door waved to Kim . "Be sure you lock the door after me. We don't want to take any chances."

Kim did as he was ordered, wondering what was in the house that had to be guarded so carefully from intruders. From behind the glass curtained window next to the front door, Kim watched Nick as he walked to his car, darting looks from side to side as he moved. Checking for tails? He'd noted Tracy doing the same when they arrived. Was this clandestine behavior really necessary? The FBI undoubtedly knew about the organization. Tracy had told Michael that the guns she stored were all licensed and legal. The FBI would most certainly have been informed. Were these student revolutionaries dramatizing themselves, following rules they'd read about in spy stories?

He turned from the window and scanned the spacious room, wondering where the weapons were stored. The furniture was plain, neat, rather featureless with its beige upholstery, cheap flowered carpet and glass-topped coffee table. No guns here. He wandered back to the window and gazed out at the tall plane trees in front of the house, their trunks like multi-colored abstract paintings. He sank onto the chair facing the front window, still staring at the bark of one of the trees. He thought of the guns Nick had said he'd have to learn how to use. If they accepted him he'd be trained as a soldier, a revolutionary. A spark of excitement shot up his spine. When he was a kid—maybe twelve or so—how he'd wanted to own a gun, like some other boys his age did. He'd tried to convince his parents to let him have one, but they were adamantly against it. He remembers feeling resentful of Dad, who'd been trained as a soldier, who'd jumped out of an airplane into the jungle, who'd had all those adventures, but who refused to have a gun in the house.

So now, if he was accepted as a member, he'd pick up his gun. Four of them. He thought of Nick, his handsome face, his self-confident air, his curiously well-groomed appearance. Had he abandoned the current style of careless dress for a more military look? No long hair, torn jeans, ragged T shirt? Kim remembered his own high school days when the Beatles, Dylan, and hippies appeared on the scene. And Timothy Leary. In no time at all most of the guys he knew took up the fashion for long hair and dirty jeans, rock and roll. And then the drugs and sex. He remembered how his parents had reacted to it all. They disapproved, of course, complaining about the music, the profane language, the ripped jeans. And the drugs, the grass, the acid? They were terrified. Mom talked about how he needed his brain, how he could become addicted, how his life could be ruined. She pictured him in an opium den. She didn't object to his long hair, at least, and she was noncommittal about his possible sexual activity. Dad gave him the talk about not getting girls into Trouble.

And there was Michael, three years older, the good student. While Kim was into the Beatles and Dylan, Michael was listening to old English folk songs and Bach. He let his hair grow a little but he still ironed his shirts and Dad didn't seem to worry about him getting some girl in trouble.

Now, Kim thought about Tracy. He grinned. That girl could get him in trouble—unlike Gina. Gentle Gina, who pleaded with him to avoid violence, who didn't understand his rage, his desire for action. He rose from the chair and straightened his shoulders. Where was Tracy, anyway? As he peered out the window onto the patio, he saw her sitting on the wooden garden bench reading the newspaper. He tapped on the window, causing her to look up. She smiled, and beckoned him to come out to her. She pointed in the direction of the kitchen. He did as she suggested and found the door, which had been left open. As he stepped onto the patio she called out to him. "So how did it go?"

"OK, I think, but Nick's going to confer with his chairman," and he sat next to her on the bench.

She gave him a steady look, her eyes a dark blue, more like the sea than the sky. "They'll probably check out what you told him."

"There shouldn't be a problem. I told the truth." He picked up her hand and fixed his eyes on hers, thinking that they were alone and had the rest of the day ahead of them, and it was time he took her to bed. He leaned forward, pressed her close and kissed her, tasting tea on her tongue. "And now, Tracy, I think it's time. . ." His fingers brushed her cheek, "that we go inside."

She laughed. "Why not?" and he led her through the kitchen door, which she locked carefully behind them before breaking into a wide smile and returning to his outstretched hand. "Let's go"

Chapter Seventeen

July, 1969, Stanford; Michael was lifting a stack of books from the cardboard box on the floor when he heard his doorbell ring. Surprised, he shoved the books onto the shelf by his desk and hurried to the door. He'd moved two days earlier to this apartment above Professor Stanton's garage. His front door was at the top of the wooden stairs that went up the side of the garage. A narrow flagstone path led to the stairs from the driveway. When Michael opened the door, Julie, his former housemate, greeted him, holding a letter in her outstretched hand. "This came for you yesterday, Michael. I thought it would be faster if I brought it over—rather than send it back to the post office."

"Oh, thanks, Julie, good of you." He looked at the handwritten return address, but couldn't make out who it was from. "Would you like to come in and see my new place? It's a mess, of course. I'm still unpacking."

Shaking her head, she turned to go. "Some other time, Michael. I have a meeting—and I'm late." She waved, trotted down the stairs and hurried to the bicycle she'd propped at the bottom. "Don't work too hard!"

Michael closed the door, slitting open the envelope as he stood there. Suddenly his heart gave a leap. He couldn't keep from smiling as he scanned the page. It was a note from Gina. . . .I'm home near Napa, she wrote, for the summer, and it's quiet and peaceful here—a contrast to the last few months in Berkeley. I've been wondering about you, and I remember that you said once that you'd like to see our vineyard, and I'm thinking, that if you'd like to come up for a visit, my family and I would like to see you. You might find the winery interesting. My Dad loves visitors to show around. Let me know if you'd like to come. Your friend, Gina.

Michael pushed aside a pile of clothes he'd dumped on the couch and sat to read the note again. She'd written her phone number at the top of the page, along with her mailing address. He folded the letter carefully, replaced it in its envelope, then pushed it into his shirt pocket. Should he accept her invitation? He wanted to, but was puzzled. What was Gina thinking?

After gazing into space for a while, rather stunned, he forced himself to move toward his box of books. While he placed the volumes on the bookshelves he thought of the conversation he'd had with his brother about Gina before Kim left with Tracy. It had followed an exchange of accusations they'd shot at one another. Michael had called Kim and his fellow-revolutionaries naïve, and Kim had countered with an attack about his work on Vietnam-war related CIA contracts. Kim had then implied that he and Gina had broken up. She was no longer his ally, he'd said. "She doesn't agree with me about how to fight the government, the establishment. She insists that peaceful protests are the only option."

"And you don't?" Michael had said.

"I think we might have to start a real revolution. With guns. We've tried everything else, haven't we?"

Michael remembered staring hard at Kim, hating to hear him talk about guns—and wanting him to say more about what happened between him and Gina. "And Gina disapproved of your going to Chicago—with Tracy and my radical housemates."

"Right. She doesn't have the guts to do more than go on a fucking march or plant a garden for peace. We used to believe in the same stuff, but not anymore."

Michael had continued to stare hard at Kim. "So now you're going to stay with Tracy. Because she stores guns at her house?"

Kim tossed him an angry look and turned on his heel. "Goodbye brother. Thanks for breakfast," and he'd marched to his car.

Michael picked up the last book in the box and squeezed it between two other thick volumes on the shelf. It was tempting to start pondering about Gina's note, wondering what he should do about it, what Kim's reaction would be, but now he must keep focused on being sharp and ready for the new job he'd start tomorrow at SRI. He'd been accepted in Douglas Engelbart's Augmentation Research Center, IT work, information technology. He hadn't told Kim about his new job, predicting that Kim would taunt him about his doing Vietnam war-connected work for the C.I.A. or the military. As far as he knew, the research being done in Engelbart's lab was still in its developmental phase. It was funded by the government, of course, ARPA money.

Picking up the empty box by the bookshelf, he glanced around the room. He noted the phone on the floor next to his desk. It hadn't been connected yet, so he couldn't call Gina from here, and he really didn't want to fool with a pay phone. Tomorrow would be soon enough to call her, anyway. The delay would force him to consider if he wanted to muddy the relationship with his brother more than it already was. What was the right way to act? He wished he had someone to talk to, to advise him. And what was Gina's motivation, anyway? Had she really given up on Kim? And what the hell was Kim doing going off with that airhead, Tracy?

The next morning Michael was up early, dressed in a clean blue shirt and khakis, and driving to his new job at SRI in Menlo Park. He approached the site with some caution, unsure if it would be picketed by demonstrators. The summer term hadn't started and most students were on a break, so he hoped there'd be a let-up of the protests. As he drove by the building, he noted a handful of young men and women marching before the main door. They held up their signs demanding cessation of DOD funding, but no one was around to read them. As Michael drove by they shouted at him and waved their signs, but he couldn't hear what they said. He eyed them warily, thinking that since Stanford had divested itself from SRI, why the hell was the place still being picketed? He'd heard that twenty-five members of Stanford's staff had left for SRI, taking eight hundred thousand dollars in contracts and 300 thousand in overhead with them.

Michael found the entrance to the parking lot, drove to the kiosk at the gate and showed the guard the letter he'd received documenting his prospective employment. He was then shown where to park his car in the spot marked for visitors. He entered a side door of the building and again presented a guard with his letter and was directed to proceed to reception. After being signed in, given his pass and his parking sticker, the attractive girl who'd helped him with the paperwork ushered him to Dr. Engelbarts lab. Her name was Melanie and she was a senior at Stanford, working as an intern for the summer, she'd confided. She'd left him at Engelbart's open door with a flirtatious smile and a "good luck!" Her eyes were shaped like Gina's, long and tilted at the corners, and for a moment he was flooded again with thoughts of Gina and Kim, but as he entered the lab's huge space he shoved those thoughts away.

He stood a second or two just inside the door, unsure of what he should do next, but soon identified who he thought might be the lab secretary seated at a desk, a typewriter before her and file cabinets at her side. As he moved toward her, he noted the enormous, metal mesh-enclosed computer against the wall at the end of the spacious room. He could hear it humming and clicking, a noise he was familiar with from his job on the campus. Scattered in front of the computer were individual small metal desks holding keyboards, printers and what looked like television monitors. Seated at chairs at each desk were four young men he assumed were programmers. On the other side of the room was a wall containing an oversized blackboard covered with chalked notations.

When he reached the desk of the graying woman he'd identified as the lab secretary, he introduced himself and handed her his folder of papers. "So you're the new recruit'" she said, smiling warmly. "I'm Mary Cook, Dr. Engalbart's secretary." She rose, and lightly touching his arm, herded him toward one of the programmers. "Dr Engalbart is at a meeting in Berkeley, but he told me to turn you over to Greg Colson. Greg will show you around. I'll check over your paperwork and get back to you. OK?"

Michael nodded a thank you and shook hands with Greg, who had hopped up from his desk. Michael guessed that Greg would be about his own age. He had bright red hair that hung in strands around his ears, wore a large blue T shirt and jeans and sandals on his feet. Michael smiled to himself, thinking that he wouldn't have to worry about his clothes while working here. He gave Greg a brief description of his background and experience with computers, and Greg led him around the room, introducing him to the three other workers and describing what was special about the main frame computer and its connections to the keyboards and monitors.

"We're working on interactive computing and user interface," he explained as they moved about. "Dr Engalbart wants to make the computer easy for anyone to use—not only expert programmers. He wants computers and people to be connected. Anywhere." As Michael stepped over the tangle of cables that connected the desk keyboards, printers, monitors to the huge computer, Greg continued. "We're developing what Doug calls the Online System, or NLS. We use interface elements like bitmapped screens, hypertext, and this gadget we call the mouse." They'd stopped in front of Greg's desk, and he picked up a two inch rectangular wooden box with a wire attached to one end. He turned the little box over, pointed to two tiny wheels, and then demonstrated how he shifted the box on a flat surface next to his keyboard. Suddenly, Michael saw a black dot moving on the screen. As Greg moved the box, the dot moved on the screen. "Far out!" Michael said, "incredible! So what do you call this gadget again?"

"A mouse. See its tail" and he tugged on the wire protruding from the end of the tiny box.

Michael put his head back and laughed. "Fantastic!" was all he could think to say. Greg then prodded him to the empty desk next to his. "You might as well get started."

"Wait," Michael said, laughing. "You mentioned a few things I know nothing about—like bit-mapped screens."

Greg clapped him on the shoulder, grinning widely. "Sure. Well, you're going to find out. Sit down. Write something."

Smiling, Michael sat down and typed two lines of code. As he typed he could hear the clicking humming sound of the computer and then the dot on the screen moving and his desk printer tapping out the code. He took a deep breath. "Amazing," he said, excitement mounting. This job was going to be a trip. Later, when Michael drove home to his new apartment after the first day of his new job, he felt a certain euphoria. The idea of connecting people to the incredible amount of information in the world was a task he'd give his eye teeth to work on. Could he find some subject to work on at the lab he could use for his dissertation? If what Engelbart claimed was true, it could really make a difference in the world, and he could be doing work that mattered, that did bring power to the people. He laughed. As he parked his car on the street and descended onto the sidewalk he gazed up at the tall pine tree growing in front of his garage apartment. The sky was a cloudless blue and robins were fluttering in and out of the pine branches. He took a deep breath and could smell the scent of jasmine growing on the fence facing the street. He found himself smiling. He felt good. He had moved to his new apartment, he'd started a new job—and maybe he'd hit on a subject for his research. And maybe for the future, so he could make his mark.

As he walked up the path toward his stairs he thought of Gina's note. Now he just had to decide what to do about his brother Kim—and Gina—and if he should call her. But had his phone been connected? He laughed. That word again. *Connected.*

Chapter Eighteen

Berkeley, July, 1969: It was a Saturday morning and as Michael drove across the bay bridge headed for his parent's house, the view of the Campanile, so clearly etched at the foot of the Berkeley hills, seemed to bid him welcome. The summer fog had burned off and it promised to be a lovely day. Sunlight had turned the hills to amber and glinted on the mildly choppy blue water of the bay. He realized he hadn't been home since his involvement in the People's Park protests, when the familiar Campanile had been enshrouded in tear gas.

Since then he'd been busy graduating, moving, starting the new job and pondering his future. He'd called Dad the evening before, wanting to talk to him about the exciting work being done at SRI. He'd also finally called Gina, suggesting he come up to Napa on Sunday—just for the day. He'd spend Saturday night at his parents. He'd promised himself to be circumspect where Gina was concerned. He'd go to Napa on a sort-of reconnaissance mission. She'd told him on the phone that she was happy he would be coming this Sunday, since she would be leaving for Italy with her mother the following week. Her mother's sister had suddenly been taken ill.

When he entered the driveway of his parents' redwood shingled house, his dog, Angus, ran toward him, yapping, a gleeful grin on his muzzle. Michael laughed as the dog jumped on him in a wild greeting. "Good boy, OK, I'm glad to see you, too!" The front door opened and Michael stepped quickly up the steps to greet Angela, who stood smiling broadly, holding out her arms for an embrace.

"Michael, it's so good to have you home. We hadn't heard from you since your graduation." Angus continued his welcoming dance as they all entered the house. "And Michael," she continued, "have you heard from Kim? Do you know where he is? He called when he returned from Chicago, but we haven't had a peep out of him since."

Michael hesitated a moment, uncertain about what to tell her, unwilling to confess his own alarm about Kim's revolutionary mood. "I'm not sure, Mom. He's in Menlo Park, staying with one of the people who went with him to Chicago." He avoided telling her Kim was staying with the girl, Tracy.

"We read about the confusion at that Chicago SDS meeting. We'd hoped to get a eye-witness report from Kim." She then took hold of Michael's arm. "Let's go out on the deck. Hank is anxious to see you. It's such a nice day. And I'll bring you some coffee."

Michael walked out the French doors that opened onto the deck and called out his greeting. Angus was still prancing at his heels. Dad put down the pen and the yellow pad he'd been working on and jumped up to give Michael a hug. "Great to see you Michael! We've missed you. Here, come and sit down."

Michael flopped onto the wooden chair opposite Hank and breathed in the scent of the eucalyptus that loomed on the slope above. It was good to be home, Angus curled up at his feet. "So how are you, Dad? Everything going OK? The new project and all."

Hank smiled. "Yeah. It's going well. It's been a change, though, believe me. Its a new field for me, but I'm working with a fine team of people. But, Michael, tell me about SRI and the lab you're in. On the phone you said Engelbart's new computer work was fantastic. So??. . ."

Leaning forward onto the table, Michael launched into his description of Engalbart's setup: the mouse, the video screen, the mainframe computer. As the words flew from his tongue, his heartbeat quickened, and Dad was listening to his every word, asking intelligent questions. How great it was to talk to him, to feel such connection. He smiled to himself. That word again.

Their excited exchange was interrupted by Angela, who was carrying a tray of coffee things toward them. Michael jumped up and took the tray from her, noting her solemn expression. He set the tray on the table and watched her as she slowly poured the coffee into three mugs. When she'd set the coffee carafe back onto the tray and handed out the mugs, she gave Hank a long, slow look. "Hank," she said finally, "I just heard on the radio—Ho Chi Minh died yesterday."

Michael felt a jolt of shock at the news, then shot a look at Hank, whose expression had darkened, his lips tightly pressed together. Angela, her eyes fixed on Hank, silently sat at the table. "Ho was 79, they said."

Still watching Hank, Michael found himself wondering if Ho's death would make any difference to the war. He'd heard pundits speculate that the Vietcong fighters might lose their will to fight without their beloved leader, but from what he'd heard from Dad he figured they'd just fight harder. "Some people," he said, his eyes on Hank, "think Ho's death would change the momentum of the war."

Hank shot him a sharp look. "This war isn't a football game, Michael. The people of Vietnam have suffered too much. They're desperate to have their freedom. Back in that jungle I watched how fiercely they handled the weapons we brought them, how quickly they learned, and marveled at the long hard hours they trained." He then fell silent again, gazing into space. Suddenly he gave a harsh laugh. "When we first landed and Ho was led out to greet us, he was so weak, so sick that he was being held up by two of his men. Our OSS team medic treated him with sulfa and quinine and God knows what else. Ho probably would have died right then if it hadn't been for the medic. Ironic, right?" He shook his head, the strange smile curling his lips. Abruptly, the smile vanished. He stared at Michael. "But I bet the men would have fought without him."

The next day Michael, in his trusty Ford, was on his way to the wine country, somewhat nervous about seeing Gina again, but still thinking about Hank's reaction to Ho Chi Minh's death. He was remembering that as a boy he'd often envied his father's WWII experiences, dreaming that he, himself was parachuting into the jungle, handling machine guns, fighting the Japs. Hank had been reluctant to talk about that time, but when he or Kim would plead for more stories, he would sometimes tell them an intriguing detail—like landing in a banyan tree or of yanking off leaches from his neck while hiking on slippery jungle trails. After America became involved in the Vietnam war he didn't speak much about his time there. They knew he believed it had been a mistake for the Americans to back the French, but he avoided the subject.

Michael remembered Angela confiding to him that since Hank was questioned by the FBI in San Francisco back in the 50's, he'd been cautious about voicing what he'd done there—or what he'd heard and seen. Michael now reminded himself that he, also, would need to be watchful concerning his security clearance. He'd been relieved when he received the letter announcing he'd been accepted for the SRI job, aware that his file would have been checked before the job was offered.

But now he had left the main highway and had reached the Napa valley. The oak dotted amber hills rose on both sides, and he was suddenly feeling the summer warmth. He considered turning on the air conditioner, but instead opened his window, allowing the sun-warmed air to blow onto his face. Gina had given him directions to the vineyard which was a few miles north of the town of Napa. Soon he spied the two-lane road heading east toward the hills. On both sides of the road he saw the long rows of grape vines bursting with clusters of fruit. In another month or so they'd be ready for harvest. He wasn't sure this was Gina's family's vineyard until he saw the sign next to a gate leading off to the right. Olivetti Winery it said. Michael's heart gave a happy lurch and he turned onto the gravel road that led through the Olivetti's fields of staked grapevines. He bumped along the road for a few yards until he was confronted by a pretty building tucked up against the slope of a hill. It looked like an Italian villa he'd seen last summer, a sprawling stone and yellow ochre stucco house roofed with red tiles and surrounded by oak trees. Bright geraniums and zinnias in terracotta pots decorated the stairways leading to it. Two large rectangular stuccoed buildings were off to the side where a variety of vehicles were parked—a large van-type truck, a couple of pickups and fork lift carriers.

Michael parked his car in the shade of an oak tree in front of the house. Before he had opened the car door, he saw Gina running down one of the stairways, followed by two golden retrievers, who barked at him but were wagging their tails. Gina greeted him with a hug and a wide smile. Michael's heart flooded with pleasure. This girl was so lovely. This place was fantastic. The air was soft, smelling of fruit and sun-drenched grass. Gina led him up the stairs, holding on to his arm, chatting merrily, excited, as if she were delighted to see him. "And Michael, my parents are waiting to meet you, and you're expected for our Sunday lunch, which my mother has been fussing over all morning."

Michael listened to her words, feeling suddenly apprehensive, rather shy. Would her family have heard about Kim? Did they think he, Michael, was her boyfriend of the moment? He'd hoped they could talk a while before meeting her parents, but apparently that wasn't going to happen. At the top of the stairs they reached a terrace overlooking the valley below, the vineyards, the opposite hills etching the horizon. Then from the open French doors a gray-haired man emerged wearing an open-necked white shirt and trousers, and who walked forward holding out his hand in a greeting. "So you are Gina's friend, Michael." His smile was broad, creasing his leathery face, displaying a gold-capped front tooth. "We were so grateful your family took Gina in during that terrible situation at the University. Giulia, my wife, spoke to your mother several times on the phone."

"My family was happy to have her," Michael said. "And it was a disturbing time."

Mr. Olivetti nodded. "Indeed. It's disturbing for all of us." Michael remembered that Gina had told him her brother, one year older, was in the navy, stationed at the moment in San Diego. "But please sit down, and will you have a glass of wine—or an aperitif?"

and he gestured to the wicker chairs on the terrace overlooking the sweeping view.

Gina, still holding Michael's arm, said hurriedly, "Papa, lunch won't be ready for another hour. I'd like to show Michael the cellars."

He gave Michael a sharp, look, as if he were judging his character. Then he smiled at Gina. "Va bene, cara, I'll wait here for you," and he settled into one of the chairs, his keen eyes following them as they descended the stairs.

Gina guided Michael to the first stone and stucco building fifty yards or so away from the house. The doors at the front of the building were tall, warehouse type, that would allow big machinery to pass inside, but Gina led him through a smaller entrance at the side. She stopped a moment, pointing to the huge space containing gleaming metal vats and rows of pipes. "My father will show you this equipment later. It's for crushing the red wine grapes. We do the white wines in the other building next door, but we don't crush them, you know. Just the juice is used. The red wines need the pulp and the skins for color."

Michael gave her a sideways glance. "No barefoot virgins? To crush the grapes in an oak vat?"

She laughed, lifting her eyebrows. "Do you think you'd find many virgins around here these days?"

"Probably not," he said with a grin, but giving her a searching look. He'd assumed that Kim and she had sex, and envied him, but Kim had never confided in him. And he did need to ask her how she felt about Kim. Maybe now was the time to broach the question. Was she available? Gina gave him a beckoning glance from the corners of her gold flecked eyes, took hold of his hand and tugged him toward a stairway going down. "The wine casks are in the cellars. That's what I want to show you. I think they're beautiful."

When they reached the bottom of the stairs he saw what she meant. A long, narrow stone cellar, arched and cool was lined on each side by rows of large oak casks. On the ends of the barrels, facing the center of the cellar, were wooden taps. The cellar smelled of wine, fermentation, cold stone. "This is the fermentation cellar, the second stage," Gina said, facing him. "Dad will show you later how they test the wine, check its chemistry—taste it. Most of the red wines are ready in one year."

He stood still, gazing about the lofty space, fascinated. "It is beautiful, Gina. So old, like a piece of ancient history." He took hold of her hand. "I can imagine hooded monks tending the wine barrels here in this stone cellar, beneath a monastery. Thank you for bringing me here." He fixed his eyes on hers, noting their openness, their depth. He wanted to touch her lovely face, make love to her. Was now the time to ask her about Kim? They both stood still for a moment, her hand in his, waiting.

Finally she answered him. I thought you'd see it, the timelessness of it. That's why I wanted you to come. . ." She paused a moment, holding his gaze. "And I guess I wanted to take this chance to explain to you what happened about Kim. I haven't heard from him since he left for Chicago, and I don't expect to see him or hear from him again. We broke up for good. I wanted to tell you that, Michael, especially now, that I'll be away for a while. When I get back I hope you'll come and visit us again." She then leaned forward, grasped his hand, and pulled him with her back up the stairs. We can't miss our lunch! My mother has been making Crespolini al Formaggio which are fantastic—and Pollo Cacciatori. And Papa has brought out his special wines. We can talk later."

"Sounds good," he said, clutching her hand, but feeling pressure in his chest, rather stunned by what she had just told him. What did Gina want from him? And did he have a chance with her? And should he? Gina pulled her hand away from his as they approached the house, where from the terrace Mr. Olivetti was watching them. He waved. Lunch was ready, he called out.

PART TWO

Chapter Nineteen

Menlo Park, August, 196; Kim pulled Tracy's blue VW bug into the driveway at the side of her house, turned off the ignition and reached to the backseat for his rifle. After slamming the car door he stood a moment, stretching his back. It had been a long day, a Friday after a long, hard week. He slung the gun over his shoulder and felt for its shells in the pocket of his jacket, checking to make sure he'd removed them as he'd been taught. By the light of the full moon he retrieved the front door key from its place under the stone, unlocked the door and returned the key, wondering if Tracy were still awake. It was late. The shooting range was only available after 10 P.M. One of the guys in their collective was the manager there and clandestinely trained them to shoot. Kim practiced with one of his four guns three nights a week for one hour. Two other nights were spent at education sessions with members of Tracy's collective. This was after his work day as a landscape gardener in Fremont—and then driving across the bay to Tracy's house. His landscaping job would be finished this coming Wednesday, thank God. His classes at Berkeley would start in two weeks.

As he walked softly into the house, he thought about what he was going to do when his classes in Berkeley started. Where would he live? He couldn't see himself returning to his parents' guest house. His parents would most certainly object to his current life, and if he were engaged in clandestine activities how could he keep it secret from them. Could he rent a room somewhere else in Berkeley or should he commute across the bay and live with Tracy? He hadn't brought up the subject to Tracy about moving in with her for an extended time. Would she consider his moving in more of a commitment than he wanted it to be?

By now he'd passed Tracy's room, and through the open door he noted that her light was off. He didn't enter but moved quietly into the room next to hers, thinking that his life was becoming increasingly complicated. And there was the subject of money. What would he do when his money ran out?

His RU collective leader talked about wanting him eventually to organize a new collective in Berkeley. They'd decided he was almost ready, that he understood the doctrine preached by Mao and the RU, and was preparing himself for the revolution. The goal, they'd said, was to rid the country of the pigs and leaders of the establishment—to cut them down—to centralize control and bring power to the people. As Mao said, Terror is a necessary weapon, not terrible, but fine. Kim wasn't committed to Mao's doctrine, but he didn't openly disagree with it. They'd told him they wanted him to take part in the next action being planned—to check him out. He turned on the light in his room, his eyes falling on the shiny cover of Mao's little red book Tracy had left on the table next to his bed. He gave it an impatient look. He had a hard time taking its catechism seriously, but he knew damned well he'd be forced to. First propping his rifle in the corner against the wall and stashing its shells into his night table drawer, he undressed and collapsed into bed.

The next morning after putting away his rifle and ammo in the locked garden shed, Kim was next to the stove cracking eggs into a bowl for scrambled eggs. Toast was in the toaster and he'd taken the butter and jam out of the fridge. He could hear that Tracy had turned off the shower and would ready for breakfast within minutes. He enjoyed fixing breakfast for Tracy on weekends. He liked to please her, show her how he appreciated her —not only in bed, but as a comrade, a fellow revolutionary. She wasn't the airhead she'd pretended to be when he first met her. She was so very different from other girls he'd known, a little crazy, and he never knew what to expect from her. There was a certain excitement in never knowing what she'd do or say next. Whether he was in love with her or not he didn't really know. Not like he'd been with Gina. If only. . . and he stopped himself. At that moment Tracy walked into the kitchen, wet hair combed back from her face, dressed in jeans and a blue T shirt. Around her fair-skinned neck she wore a thin gold chain. He turned and gave her a quick kiss. "Scrambled eggs coming up!" he said.

"Mmm good, I'm hungry," and she moved to the toaster and placed the four pieces of toast that had popped up into a small basket. "Nick and Kevin will be here soon," she said, glancing at the clock. "We need to go over our stuff."

That evening, a few miles away on the Stanford campus, Michael hung up his phone. He'd been talking to his parents, who had been asking him to try to contact Kim. "We haven't heard from him in over a month," Angela had said, her voice thick with worry. "And Michael you work in Menlo Park and Kim lives there somewhere, but he hasn't given us his phone number or address. Please find him and tell him there's a stack of mail here for him, some from the university, and remind him classes start soon."

Michael stared at the phone, experiencing mixed emotions—concern for his parents, irritation with Kim, but at the same time, concern for him, too. And there was the question of Gina. She'd been in Italy and he hadn't seen her since the Sunday afternoon he'd visited her at the winery, but he had a date with her next week in Berkeley. He'd been considering talking to Kim about Gina, but knew it would be fucking difficult. He'd put off that conversation, but maybe now was the moment for it to happen while the sound of his mother's distraught voice still echoed in his ears.

He'd already thought about calling Julie, who would undoubtedly know where her friend Tracy lived, and where he knew Kim was staying, but he'd put that off, too. But now was the time. Resolved, he picked up the phone and dialed Julie's number, which he knew quite well, of course. Ron answered, and after a short exchange of news, which wasn't much except that Alistair had moved out, too, Julie came on the line. After a moment's hesitation she said yes, she had Tracy's phone number—and her address,"over on Princeton

Road, not far from SRI." Michael flashed on the day when Tracy told him about the guns she stored in her house. Did Julie feel somewhat disloyal at providing her address? Michael jotted it down, thanked her, agreed they all had to get together soon, and hung up the phone. He glanced at his watch. It was still early, 7:30. He put his hand on the phone and then changed his mind. No, he wouldn't call. He'd go to Tracy's house, knock on the door and maybe Kim would be home, maybe not, but if he waited the strength of his resolve might weaken.

He found Princeton Road without difficulty. It was in an older section of Menlo where large homes were sheltered by a variety of mature, leafy trees. The buildings were set back from the street behind manicured gardens. To his surprise, Tracy's house was not unlike the others on this tree-lined street. He had expected to find a run-down commune, a pad. Instead he was faced with a well-kept Tudor-style house shaded by plane trees. A neat brick path led to a heavy oak door complete with an antique brass door-knocker. Michael tapped it a couple of times and then noticed the button for a bell, which he pushed. After a moment he realized the curtain covering the window next to the door was being twitched aside. He smiled, wondering if who ever was peering at him would let him in. Soon he heard the click of locks turning, and the door was yanked opened by Tracy, who gave him a beaming smile. "Michael! What the hell are you doing here? Checking up on your little brother?"

Michael laughed. "Yeah, Tracy. I've been wondering what happened to him. Is. he here?"

"Sure, Michael. He's here. Come on in. He's in the kitchen." She opened the door wide, ushering him inside and then locked it from inside. He glanced quickly around the room, noting it's simple, plain furnishings, a contrast to the house's upscale exterior. He followed Tracy who called out to Kim, a warning tone in her voice, "Michael's here to see you."

Kim looked up, startled "Michael, for Christ's sake, what's up?" He moved a step forward, smiling nervously.

Michael noted Kim's edginess and attempted a reassuring smile. "Nothing much, Kim. So how are you?" He drew closer but didn't attempt a hug. "It's just that Mom called, worried about you. Says she has a stack of mail for you. Some from the university. It might be important."

Kim seemed unable to reply, but Tracy came to the rescue "Come on, guys. How about some tea? I just made a fresh pot. Then let's go to the other room."

She tossed Kim a sharp glance and Kim snapped to attention. "Good idea. He reached into a cabinet, brought out three mugs, and set them on the counter. "I've been busy. Michael." Tracy then poured tea and they all moved toward the living room. Kim continued. "I've been working in Fremont for the landscape architect, John Stone—commuting every day."

Michael settled onto one of the chairs while Kim and Tracy sat next to each other on the couch. "So, Michael, how's Mom? I'm sorry she's worried about me. It's just—well, that I've been up to my neck with stuff. I'll call her. And Dad?"

"They're both fine, Kim, just concerned about you, wondering what you're up to. I hadn't heard from you either." He reached for his wallet, pulled out a card and scribbled his new address and phone number on the back. "And here's my new address and phone number."

Kim put the card in his shirt pocket and took a sip of tea, giving Tracy a quick glance. "I guess I've just been working my ass off. Putting in a garden is tough work, believe me, and commuting is a fucking nightmare." He set his cup on the table next to the couch and put his arm around Tracy's shoulders. "And what about you? You were about to move when I last saw you. And starting a new job. At SRI, no less, the heart of darkness." He raised his eyebrows. "Funded by the U.S. government?"

Michael gave a short laugh. "Yeah, I moved onto campus and I'm working at an SRI computer lab—funded by the government—nothing evil, brother. In fact, my boss wants to bring power to the people—with personal computers."

Tracy burst into a loud laugh. "Far out, Michael! Insane!" She extricated herself from Kim's arm and hopped onto her feet. "OK,

I'll leave you two guys. I have letters to write." She waved and flitted out of the room, still laughing.

Michael watched her lithe movements as she closed the hall door behind her, thinking that now was the time for him to bring up the subject of Gina. He turned back to Kim, focusing on his face. He had a strained look, seeming pale under his tan, and his eyes were shadowed. Maybe he was working too hard. And fucking Tracy as well?

Kim returned his scrutinizing look. "Well, Michael, and how are you? Got your draft deferral OK?"

"Yeah, thank God. I got it. I'm a grad student and doing government work. And by the way, Mom said to remind you Cal classes start in two weeks."

"Shit, Michael. I know. I just don't know where I'll be staying." He sighed deeply.

Michael stared at him. "Not at home?"

"Not sure. Maybe here with Tracy."

Michael let out a sharp breath. Maybe Kim was truly over Gina. OK, now was the time. "Kim, I heard from Gina a month or so ago—before she left for Italy—and I went to see her up at the winery."

"Oh, so how's she doing?" Kim's tone was casual, as if he were talking about a person he knew in another life.

Michael plunged. "She's fine. She and her mother are at her Aunt's villa near Milan at the moment. The aunt had a stroke and Gina's mother wanted to be with her. Gina will be back next week—time for classes to begin. As a matter of fact I have a date with her in Berkeley the Saturday before school starts."

Kim gave him a long, studied rather surprised look, as if he were trying to fit what Michael was telling him with his view of the person he thought Michael was—and was having trouble putting it all together. He finally spoke. He said slowly, "so you and Gina are dating?"

Michael held his look. "Well. . . I have a date with her week after next. When I saw her up in Napa we got along great. And I'm pretty sure I want to see her again—if she agrees. And I guess I want to know if you're OK with that. . ."

Kim's eyes flickered a moment before he broke eye contact and stared out the front window, as if trying to make sense of what he'd just heard. He shrugged, turned, and gave a wry laugh. "Hell, Michael, if you want to date her, whatever, don't mind me! I thought I loved her once, but not any more. She used to love me, too, but she was turned off by what I'd become. Now we don't look at the world the same. She's too gentle for me, too nice." He stood up and peered down at Michael, his gray eyes as hard as cement. "I changed, you know. I changed when that cop split my head open and when the blue meanies stomped on me. Gina? Go ahead, brother, make your move, if you want. It won't bother me. I have too much on my plate right now. I feel like I have the whole, fucking world pressing on me."

A surge of compassion for his brother pulled Michael to his feet. Kim was really in trouble. "I wish I could think of something to say to help you feel less angry, Kim, but I can't—except stay away from cops and jails from now on. Go back to school!"

Kim shrugged, his expression softening. "Yeah, I will. Go back to school, at least. Probably. And Michael, say hello to Gina when you see her. OK? And no hard feelings."

"OK. No hard feelings." He was about to give Kim a brotherly hug, but at that moment Kim moved toward the front door as if he were expecting Michael to leave. Michael took the hint and stepped to the door. It had been an emotional exchange and they both needed a break. He just hoped Kim was telling the truth about his feelings for Gina being over. "Well, Kim, let's get together again, soon. And say goodbye to Tracy for me. Bye, Kim. Take it easy, dude."

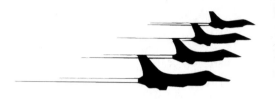

Chapter Twenty

San Francisco, September,1969; Michael and Gina glided down the steps at the Opera House, both humming Mimi's aria from La Boheme, Gina swaying as if she were dancing to the melody, her eyes shining. Michael felt as if he were floating at her side, a crazy happiness carrying him aloft. At the bottom of the steps he reached to kiss her, his arm tightly wound around her waist, unconcerned about their blocking the people descending the stairs behind them. Gina tossed him a sideways, radiant glance, pressing his hand against her side, still humming. "Albanese sang like an angel, didn't she? I heard her here two years ago in Butterfly, but this was fantastic." She leaned her head on his shoulder. "How did you know I love Puccini operas?"

Michael laughed. "I didn't, Gina. I just guessed you love opera—like I do—and I saw in the paper La Boheme was on tonight. I was lucky to get good tickets." He'd figured that her family being from Italy she'd be bound to be an opera lover. They sauntered arm in arm to the parking lot and climbed into his car where he'd parked it after driving across the bridge from Berkeley. Now they would head for Lupo's in North Beach, where Gina told him she loved to go for canoli, a Sicilian dessert. "They have good pizza, too, if you're hungry."

After an irritating search for a parking place, they finally arrived at Lupo's—only to find a line of customers waiting for a table. Gina shrugged. "Sorry, Michael, but it's well worth waiting for." They took their place in line, standing behind another young couple. When the man turned to speak to his girl, Michael let out a cry of surprise. "Alistair! So how are you? I haven't seen you since you left for home in June." Alistair's hair had been cut so that it fell just above is shirt collar, and his jacket and slacks were neatly pressed.

Alistair turned and clapped Michael on the shoulder. "Hey. Michael, how's it going. So what are you doing up in the big city?"

"We just went to the opera." Michael said, his arm around Gina's waist.

"Well, for Christ's sake, so did we." Since Michael noted that the girl with Alistair was not Julie, he refrained from mentioning Julie's name. Had they broken up? It was hard to keep up with these relationships. Lovers weren't always constant, as he well knew, but at that moment he was certain that he was so much in love with Gina, he'd love her forever. The two former housemates then introduced their dates. Alistair's girl, Sara Finn, a blue-eyed brunette was also a student at Stanford, Alistair explained. "And, Michael, you moved, I hear—and so did I. Julie and Ron found new housemates." He touched Sara's hand. "I share a house with two other students and Sara."

Michael grinned. "Sounds good! I'm on my own now," and he described his room over the Professor's garage. He eyed Gina, considering how much he wished she were his roommate. She looked so lovely tonight, in her emerald green silk shift and black velvet jacket. The soft candle light in the restaurant glimmered on her gold hoop earrings and lit the amber flecks in her eyes. He'd noted Alistair's approving glance when he'd introduced her.

By now the people waiting ahead of them had been seated, and the maitr'd approached them suggesting he had a booth for four if they would like to take it. Michael exchanged glances with the others and they agreed. Michael had felt a moment's hesitation. He'd preferred to have Gina alone, but since the place was so crowded. . . they soon found themselves seated together in a well-used oak booth toward the back of the room. After ordering glasses of wine, a three-cheese pizza to share and canoli, Alistair gave Michael a questioning look. "Michael, so how's Kim? I haven't seen him since Chicago.

Julie told me he'd crashed at Tracy's place in Menlo. Will he go back to Berkeley?"

Michael shot a glance at Gina, wondering how she would react to hearing Kim's name. He'd already told her that Kim was with Tracy, and she hadn't shown any sign of displeasure at hearing it—and didn't now. He turned back to Alistair and shrugged. "I hope he'll be in Berkeley for classes next week, but I'm not sure what he's going to do."

"Did he tell you about what happened in Chicago?"

"Yeah. Really wild, right?"

"And how! SDS fell apart. And those Chicago Panthers—Jeez, what a fuck up."

"So did you go with the new version of SDS, with what's-her-name?"

"Dohrn? No, I don't like the direction they're taking—the Weathermen and stuff, but I'm working on the march planned for October. Non-violent, the Vietnam Moratorium. We just have to keep up the protests. I don't believe for one minute that Nixon is telling the truth about his negotiations with Hanoi and his statements about reducing troop numbers. What he does keep saying is that though he wants to reduce the troops, he's not ready to remove them—because we can't be seen by the world as weak. And I keep hearing stories about B-52 bombings of Cambodia and Laos—and plans to mine the Gulf—and bomb the shit out of north Vietnam cities. And that snake Kissenger's always at Nixon's side, and you know he's whispering into Nixon's ear—like an Iago, telling him lies."

Michael nodded, finding that he agreed with Alistair, who seemed to have abandoned his hyper-radical leanings. Had Alistair broken up with Julie because of her involvement with that Maoist group, the one Professor Franklin supported? At that moment the waiter arrived with their pizza and four plates, promising to bring the canoli later. The conversation then switched away from politics to discussing the opera and plans for the coming school year. Michael described his

136

excitement about Engelbart's idea for personal computer use. Finally, the canoli was consumed, which they all agreed was fantastic.

It was almost two A.M. when the two couples left Lupos together and walked along the North Beach Barbary Coast street, laughing as they passed Finochios, Gina and Sara giggling as they stared at the man in drag calling the passers-by to "come see the last show!" Then, Alistair was pointing down the side street, "My car is this way, so Michael, it's been good to see you." He tugged a card from his wallet and scribbled a phone number on the back. "Let's get together soon, OK?" Michael nodded, promising to call him, and giving a wave he draped his arm around Gina's shoulders and they headed for his car.

Although he was tempted to suggest Gina come with him to his room at Stanford, he decided against it. It was too soon to make that move. He'd take her back to her co-op in Berkeley. He was in love, but would try not to rush her. What an incredible night!

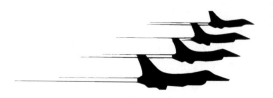

Chapter Twenty-One

Berkeley, December 20 1969; The sky was darkening by the time Kim reached his parents' house. He parked Tracy's VW in the driveway, ran up the front steps and opened the door, which was unlocked, as usual. Angus pranced out to greet him, yelping, jumping, as if it had been years since he'd been home. "Good boy, Angus," Kim said, ruffling the dog's thick fur, "I know, it's been a while." And it was true. He hadn't been home much this semester, and then only to pick up his mail or when he drove his old porcupine VW home and left it in the garage. Tracy had driven him back to Menlo in her new Datsun. He'd brought Tracy home to meet his parents and they obviously didn't think much of her, although she followed his entreaties to stay off politics, RU and gun collections.

He'd promised to have dinner with his parents tonight, since he couldn't come home for Christmas. He'd lectured himself to refrain from explosive topics of discussion. The last time he'd been home he and Dad had fought bitterly about almost everything, And even Mom disapproved of his nouveau radicalism, as she called it. Mom's opinion of Tracy didn't improve when he told her he wouldn't come for Christmas because Tracy had pressured him to help her cooking for the poor on that day.

Now he peered into the living room, but finding it empty shouted, "anyone home?" He then caught the aroma of sautéd onions wafting from the kitchen, and as he moved in that direction, he heard Mom calling his name. She hurried toward him and hugged him hard. "It's so good to have you home, Kim. We miss you. Hank will be here soon. Come, sit down, while I finish this salad," and she moved to the kitchen counter where she'd been chopping celery. "Oh, and you have more mail. It's on the table by the front door. It's. . ." and she paused, a shadow crossing her face. "Kim, it's from the Selective Service."

"Oh?" He felt the hit those words always caused, but it lasted only a second. "Maybe it's telling me what my lottery draft number is—but we already know that, so don't worry, Mom. Number 127 isn't too bad, and I still have my student deferral anyway." He moved toward the mail table cursing the government for dreaming up this new torture device, the lottery. They claimed that people accused local draft boards of racial and class bias in their selections. Supposedly, they said, the dreaded lottery would be a method to increase the fairness of the draft. Shit, as far as he was concerned, it made it worse.

He'd tried to sound reassuring to Mom, but now his hand trembled as he opened the letter. Fortunately it said nothing he didn't already know. He'd seen the published list as soon as it came out in the paper the day after the December first lottery two weeks ago. It blew his mind to think that his fate depended on that tiny piece of paper in the blue capsule with his birthday written on it, the luck of the draw, for sure. His heart still hammered as he recalled staring at the picture of the glass container with its 363 blue plastic capsules ready to be drawn. He'd peered through a fog of dread as he scanned the list of birth dates and draft numbers. He also remembers the prick of envy he'd felt when he read Michael's number—315, which probably meant Michael wouldn't get drafted. His own number, 127, could be called at the end of the year. It would be convenient to believe that Nixon was telling the truth about how the troops would soon be withdrawn and the war be over. However, that snake could most definitely not be trusted. His so-called peace talks in Paris were just a sham.

Now he stuffed the letter into the back pocket of his jeans, and as he headed to the kitchen, he heard the sound of footsteps on the back steps and watched his Dad opening the door. He noted how Hank's face lit up when they made eye-contact, and then quickly looked away, covering his confusion by fending off Angus's enthusiastic greeting. "OK, Angus, I need to say hello to Kim," and he stepped forward and touched him lightly on the shoulder. "It's good to see you, Kim."

Angela was watching them both, her hands gripping the back of a chair at the kitchen table. She gave a nervous smile, and Hank moved behind her and kissed the back of her cheek. "Dinner isn't quite ready," she said, her eyes fixed on Hank. "Why don't you bring out some wine, Hank. And let's go into the living room and relax a while."

"Sure," Hank said, struggling out of his padded nylon jacket and tossing it on a chair in the corner. "You're twenty-one now, Kim. We can serve you legally." Kim gave a polite laugh and watched as Hank opened the cupboard where he kept the wine. "And, Kim, I see there's a blue VW parked in the driveway. Yours?"

"Not exactly. It's Tracy's. She loaned it to me after she bought her new car, a Datsun, so I'd have something reliable to drive. Remember, I brought my old porcupine VW and parked it in the garage. That was when you met Tracy. The car had problems. I drove it too much last summer when I was going to Fremont every day." Kim noted how his parents exchanged quick looks, as if he had said something significant. Tracy hadn't given him the car. It was registered in her name, and she had her new car, but she insisted he use the VW to get to school and to his job, and of course, to do the organizing he was supposed to be doing for RU.

Hank was eying him, speculatively. "It sounds as though Tracy has money to spare. She's from Texas, you told us?"

"Yeah, she's from Texas. Oil money. A trust fund. But, Dad, she's not your usual rich girl. . ." He stopped himself from continuing. How could he explain Tracy to them? How could he explain her to himself! She was using her money to support a revolution. She was a Maoist, for Christ's sake, which he'd been trying to talk her out of, actually, but she truly believed in sharing the wealth with the people. If he tried to get them to understand Tracy, they'd be yelling at each other again. And he certainly couldn't mention the Revolutionary Union.

Hank had poured three glasses of Merlot, handed Angela and Kim theirs, and then picking up the wine bottle and his own glass ushered them into the living room. After they were all seated, he lifted his glass. "Cheers, it's good to have you home, Kim."

They all drank, and after Angela took her sip of wine, she turned to Kim. "What I can't figure out, Kim, is why you need to be so independent. I can understand why you prefer to room with your girlfriend, but why do you refuse financial help from us? We could help you pay for a car! Instead you'll be beholden to Tracy." She paused and gave him a scrutinizing look "And I think you're working too hard. How many hours do you put in a week at that architect's firm?"

"About fifteen. It's not so bad, Mom, and it fits in fine with my studio work. I've been able to keep up with most of my classes, and I need to learn about what goes on at the construction site. Our architects work with Newman, the builder of modern, single-family homes. Lots of glass, light, openness, slab floors with radiant heating. I'm learning a lot about how it all works." And he wouldn't tell her how he was supposed to be organizing the construction workers for an RU cell, which wasn't getting anywhere anyway.

Angela was still staring at him, as if she wanted question him further, but was hesitating. He took a gulp of wine, trying to think of something else to say that wouldn't lead to argument. Then he thought of asking about Michael. "So, what do you guys hear from Michael? I haven't talked to him for a couple of weeks. He's seeing a lot of Gina, apparently."

Angela nodded. "Yes, last weekend they came by. A nice girl." She gave him another sharp look. "You and Gina broke up, I understand. Amicably?"

"Yeah. We just decided we didn't see eye to eye on a lot of things. I guess I changed after I got hit and arrested. I was so angry. . ." He stopped himself. This was dangerous territory. He took a sip of wine, searching for something else to talk about. Finally, he blurted,

"Michael is really happy with his work at Engelbart's lab, he tells me. He's found some problem he can work on for his dissertation."

Hank, who had been quietly listening to the exchange between Angela and Kim, leaned forward. "Yes, and it's an interesting one, and could be important," and he proceeded to explain the subject in considerable detail. As Kim concentrated on Dad's analysis of Michael's work, he relaxed, realizing that the subject intrigued Hank. It was something new and had no political implications—it was safe territory.

Angela then rose from her chair and excused herself. "The pot roast should be ready. I'll call you when it's done," and she picked up her wine glass and headed for the kitchen. Kim took a deep breath. Maybe he could get through this evening without blowing it, after all.

Chapter Twenty-Two

April, 1970, Stanford; Michael finished work on his program for the day and sauntered to the parking lot. Glancing at his watch, he noted he had plenty of time to get to the Oasis, the student hangout a mile or so beyond the campus. He'd promised to meet Alistair there for beer and hamburgers at 5:30 that evening. He and Alistair had become good friends since their accidental meeting after the opera at the beginning of the fall semester, about six months ago. Their meeting place this evening, the Oasis, displayed a large TV screen over the bar, normally used for watching football games, but recently had become a popular place to watch news from Vietnam and the protests. Nixon was giving a speech tonight that promised to be controversial.

As Michael climbed into his car he smiled when he eyed the cap Gina had left on the dashboard during the Easter holiday weekend two weeks earlier. The sight of the cap lifted his spirits, turned his thoughts away from the world of work and war. He maneuvered his car into the traffic thinking about how Gina had been able to spend three precious days with him that week. They'd spent a lot of it in bed, but had managed to go to the beach for a day—Pescadero, over the hill from Stanford, and to lunch at Duarte's, a venerable bay area tavern run by the Duarte family for over seventy years. Gina had been delighted with old Mrs Duarte who reigned over the dining room with warmth and humor. After lunch they'd walked on the beach at low tide, searching for starfish in the tide pools. The air smelled of salt and seaweed, and he remembers Gina looking like a mermaid, her long hair flying in the fresh breeze and how he kissed her, holding her close, their bare feet in the cold water, sand creeping between their toes. Thinking about that moment caused his chest to expand. He was happy, imagine! The world was in a mess but he felt wonderful.

But now he was approaching the Oasis, another tavern— not known for its culinary prowess, but it was the cool place to hang with your friends. He'd met Alistair here two weeks ago and Alistair had been feeling discouraged about the weakness of the response to the last Vietnam Moratorium protest. He and Michael were both against the war, but opposed to violent acts of protest—the trashing of windows, the bombing of ROTC buildings—and especially groups like the Weather Underground, who were responsible for a growing number of bombings throughout the country.

When Michael walked through the door into the roadside tavern he spied Alistair sitting at one of the scarred wooden tables in good viewing distance of the TV, a large pitcher of beer before him and two beer mugs. They greeted each other with a wave and Michael sat on the bench opposite him. "So, how's it goin' Alistair? Are you ready for what our great leader is about to lay on us?"

Alistair snorted. "Yeah, it'll be nothing good, for sure." He then pushed himself up from the table and suggested they put in their order for food at the bar. "The place is already filling up. There've been those reports about Cambodia bombings—and the coup—and nobody trusts that snake Nixon."

Rising from the bench, Michael nodded. "You never know what he's going to say next—or what's worse—what he's going to do next."

After ordering their hamburgers and fries they returned to their table and Alistair poured them each a full mug of beer. Michael took a long swallow of the cold beer. It had been a warm day for April, and the liquid slid down his throat, smooth and delicious. He glanced around the table-filled room, which were now all occupied by shaggy haired guys in jeans, girls in short, short skirts and long shining hair. More young people pressed through the doors and stood at the bar. He had to lean forward to hear Alistair, who was talking again about what was happening to Vietnam Moratorium. "We've just about given up on peace marches. They haven't worked—and the last one was a fizzle. Guys are discouraged—or maybe they believe Nixon when they hear him talking about withdrawing troops."

The noise in the room continued to mount and Michael responded with only a nod. He hesitated to yell out his anti-war opinions even here with this bunch of students. FBI agents were probably sitting at the next table. He glanced over his shoulder and drank his beer. He remembers too well Hank's stories about his being questioned by the FBI.

When the sound decreased somewhat, he leaned close to Alistair, and in a low tone said, "no, I don't have an answer. You're right, the news continues to be bad. In spite of all the promises." He glanced over his shoulder again and leaned even closer. "And last week there were the reports of the coup in Cambodia. While King Sihanouk was on vacation in France. An anti-communist took over."

"Right," Alistair said, also speaking quietly, "Lon Nol. And there've been those stories of B 52 bombings of the North Vietnamese sanctuaries there by our air force."

Michael nodded. What was going on, he wondered. Was the CIA involved in the coup? Were we now backing this guy, Lon Nol? Who was he, anyway?

Suddenly, a wave of silence descended on the room and the bartender turned up the sound on the TV. A newscaster was announcing that the President was about to speak. The camera panned to the Oval Office, the American flag and to the presidential desk where Nixon ceremoniously took his seat before the microphone. Michael exchanged looks with Alistair, who raised his eyebrows and folded his arms on his chest. As the camera focused on Nixon's face, hisses and boos bounced around the room. Michael noted the President's skin, slick with sweat, his mouth in a wide, toothy smile—a crocodile smile. *Good evening my fellow Americans:* Nixon began. The yells and hisses ceased and the crowd seemed to hold it's collective breath.

Ten days ago, in my report to the Nation on Vietnam, I announced a decision to withdraw an additional 150,000 Americans from Vietnam over the next year. I said then that I was making that decision despite our concern over increased enemy activity in Laos, in Cambodia, and in South Vietnam. At that time, I warned that if I concluded that increased enemy activity in any of these areas endangered the lives of Americans remaining in Vietnam, I would not hesitate to take strong and effective measures to deal with that situation.

A low rumbling of voices now broke the silence. Michael glanced around the room, noting the tense mouths and focused eyes of his fellow watchers. The words *strong measures* had caught their attention.

Nixon then moved frm his desk to a board showing a map of Cambodia. He pointed to what he called the North Vietnam sanctuaries along the Vietnam/Cambodian border, describing the base camps, airstrips used for hit and run attacks on American forces. He paused, and staring straight into the camera said, *for five years, neither the United States nor South Vietnam has moved against these enemy sanctuaries because we did not wish to violate the territory of a neutral nation.*

The room exploded. "Liar!" they yelled, "Hypocrite! Bullshit, bullshit" drowning out Nixon's words. They finally quieted enough to hear Nixon's droning voice, but continued to yell out their anger and disbelief, and when he came to the point of his speech at last and said, *In cooperation with the armed forces of South Vietnam, attacks are being launched this week to clean out major enemy sanctuaries on the Cambodian-Vietnam border.*

After a moment of stunned silence, as the meaning of Nixon's words hit home, a roaring tornado couldn't have sounded more ferocious. On their feet, more than half the audience, both men and women, howled their dissent, their rage. They stormed out the door shouting "End the war NOW." Michael and Alistair looked at each other, then solemnly watched them leave. "All hell is breaking loose," Michael said, quietly. "Where will it end?"

The two men rose and slowly followed the throng, each heading for his car. Michael stopped his car at the edge of the parking lot until the people ahead of him had crowded into vehicles, their heads poking from the windows shouting out their rage as they drove toward the Stanford campus. Within minutes Michael heard the wailing of police sirens, and as he turned onto Campus Drive not far from his apartment, he could hear the clamor from the center of campus, the sounds blaring from loudspeakers of voices, static, the drumbeat of rock and the answering shouts from a horde of students. He drove slowly along the street, forced to zigzag through the jam of students rushing from their dorms or fraternity houses, heading for the quad. Some were carrying hastily made signs with the word STRIKE held aloft.

Michael's gut tightened and his heart beat faster. He parked his car, and instead of climbing the stairs to his apartment he turned toward the eye of the storm, pulled as if by a riptide in a turbulent sea. Electricity sparked in the air and although he was drawn by the excitement, the drama, he also felt a heavy sense of dread in a cave somewhere deep inside. Damn that Nixon! Why did he do it? What did he think he'd accomplish!

Michael found himself in a crush of people pressing into the quad. The old student union seemed to be the headquarters for the revolt. Students were lugging tables and chairs outside the building, piling them into a barricade around it. A line of marchers carrying strike signs chanted anti-war slogans. Speakers at a make-shift platform yelled into a microphone, their voices drowned out by the shrieks of the police sirens and the sounds of breaking glass as another line of students swept through the campus, throwing rocks at windows as they rushed by. Michael retreated. This wasn't his scene. What did it accomplish? He turned and pushed his way through the crowd away from the quad. As he stumbled away, he caught a glimpse of Julie in the herd, shouting with the others, her face contorted with anger. He thought of Kim and then of Tracy, wondering how the radicals would be reacting to this latest Nixon betrayal. Then he thought of Gina. Berkeley would be a war zone, for sure, and Gina's co-op was in the center of it. When he got home he grabbed his phone and dialed her number. She answered immediately, assuring him that she was fine, "I'll just stay put. I can watch what's happening from my window. And I can hear the sirens. So far no riot police on the street—and no tear gas, but it's early!" She gave a shaky laugh. "But can you believe that Nixon! He called us students "bums" blowin' up the campuses. And I heard on KFBK that our bombers were raining bombs down on Hanoi and other cities filled with people!"

He could hear the tremor in her voice as she spoke but couldn't think of anything to say to her to make her feel better. He knew how powerless she felt, how uncertain, and he wanted to be with her. They agreed that they'd meet as soon as they could figure out how. Both Berkeley and Stanford would be on strike. Classes would shut down. Michael figured that his lab at SRI would still function, but the class he taught as a TA at the Applied Electronics Center would be canceled for sure.

That night he barely slept. Tensely he listened to the tumult; sirens shrieking, cars racing, yelling on the streets—all which continued the next day—and the next, when a university strike was started. Pickets and protesters blocked entrances to buildings, stopping students and faculty from entering. Although Michael biked to work at SRI, he didn't even try to go to the class he taught, and in the next few days as he watched news reports on TV and witnessed what was happening on campus, he knew that Stanford's President Pitzer had extended the strike and all but the administrative offices were closed. Governor Reagan closed the entire state university system, and when four students were killed and eight wounded at Kent State by National Guardsmen, universities all over the country went on strike and closed their doors. And nothing changed. The bombs kept dropping and soldiers kept dying.

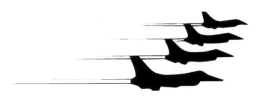

Chapter Twenty-Three

enlo Park, June,1970; Kim switched off the living room television and sat for a moment trying to organize his thoughts. He could hear Tracy in the bedroom talking on the newly installed phone with Nick, who would be coming here for a meeting in another hour. The last time he'd been here he'd said the action their collective had planned was important. Something different. They must escalate the fight against capitalist, imperialist governments that exploited the international working class. "We are terrorists," Nick had said, "like Mao told us to be. The armed revolution must begin—now, while the country is seething with anger about the war, the killing of third world people, and the student deaths at Kent State." Nervously, Kim wondered what Nick and the others had planned. He wanted change, of course, but he wasn't at all sure he wanted to be a terrorist for Mao.

He rose from the couch and scanned the room, considering the possibility that the house was bugged. Nick had hinted that since the pigs knew about the guns in the shed, the FBI might have been alerted. Was Nick being overly cautious, caught up in the drama of the revolutionary, exaggerating his own importance? He thought of what Michael had said about revolutionaries the last time they'd talked. They're caught up in the drama, he'd said, the rhetoric, the excitement of engaging in dangerous acts. Kim stared at the blank TV screen. It was hard to know what to think, but it made sense to be cautious. Nick could be right about the house being bugged. He'd said that they should go outside somewhere, like on the patio, to talk about any proposed clandestine action.

And so an hour later, when Nick and Kevin, a Stanford communications major, turned up they all trooped out to the patio and sat around a round redwood picnic table. Kim had noted that Nick had been carrying a Pan Am flight bag when he first arrived, but before joining them at the table had disappeared into the wooden shed behind the patio for a few moments, returning empty handed. The shed contained the cache of guns the collective had been storing. Kim wondered what had been in the flight bag, a hand gun? He glanced behind him at the trellised wall of the windowless shed that formed the fourth wall of the patio. The trellis was covered in California honeysuckle, which was in full bloom and sweetly fragrant.

Now Nick flipped back a lock of his blond hair, and began to unroll a large sheet of paper which he set on the table before them. He nailed each one of them with a sharp look as he tapped the paper. "The date of the next action is one week from tonight. We have to move quickly. We must show our rage at Nixon's invasion of Cambodia—and the bombing of third world cities and villages. And. . ." with a slight, crooked smile, said, "take advantage of the cops being occupied by rock-throwing students breaking windows. We'll have less time than usual for planning, but if we all concentrate, keep our heads clear we'll succeed."

Resuming his stern expression, he smoothed the paper, which seemed to be a scaled drawing of a building set within a sketch of the streets around it. "OK, this is our target—the Bank of America next to the La Fonda shopping mall in Belmont."

Kim tried not to show his shock at what he'd just heard, but his rib cage had constricted and his heart was thudding. Bombing the Bank of America? He fixed his eyes on Nick's face as he spoke. His eyes had hardened, but his voice was calm and he spoke clearly and directly, as if he were organizing a fund-raising event—assigning tasks to each member. "Kim, you're to do surveillance of the exterior of the building, noting entrances, exits, workers schedules, deliveries, trash pickups, anything that could be of use when deciding where to plant the bomb." He turned to Tracy. "Tracy, you're to watch the inside of the bank, the employees, their schedules, hours of operation and the numbers of customers and their behavior." He paused, and gave his three listeners sharp looks. "The building must be unoccupied when it's blown. Nobody must be killed." His blue eyes peered at them sternly,

For a moment Kim stopped breathing, but he couldn't keep himself from blurting, "and IF someone is killed? What happens then? Nick. . . ?"

Nick gave him a hard, cold look. "Kim, you and Tracy will make certain that the bank is empty. It's imperative that no one is killed or injured. That's why it's so important that you do a precise surveillance of the bank's traffic and schedules. It's up to you to make sure nobody, absolutely nobody, is killed or hurt. We must avoid having our people arrested. We can't complete our mission if our comrades are in jail—or on death row."

Kim didn't find these words comforting. He was still in shock, rather numb, but he found himself listening carefully. It was a question of discipline, of organization, of forcing his brain to control his emotions. Nick then turned to Kevin, the Communication major, the technical expert with radio and TV. "Kevin, you will gather the materials to make the bomb and put it together. My job is to give you whatever assistance you need and to watch Kim and Tracy's backs." He paused, took a deep breath, eying the trellised wall behind him. "And Kevin, I've put the C4 plastic explosive in the gun shed. It's in the Pan Am airline bag. It's safe there, but be careful with it, everyone," and he shot each of them a warning look. "And Kevin, there's also a 9V battery, an alarm clock for the timing device and plenty of electrical wire. You'll need a detonator. Talk to Bruce. He'll know who might have one."

Kevin nodded, his brown eyes glinting. "OK. If I can't find a manufactured detonator, I might be able to rig up something with a door buzzer or some such gadget."

Nick raised his eyebrows. "Let's hope you can get a real one, Kevin, but you know what you're doing." He folded the drawing that had been spread on the table and handed it to Kim. "You should copy this and use it to note significant details about the building and its traffic. We'll meet again here Thursday night to finalize our plan of action." He looked at Kevin, determination in his eyes. "By then the bomb will be ready, right?"

"Right!" Kevin said, grinning. Then—'bye 'bye bank!"

As Kim scanned the intent faces of his three companions, his fear began to diminish. His hands had stopped shaking. Instead, a rush of excitement zipped up his spine. They'd actually do it! Instead of attacking the military or government facilities, they would be going directly to its controlling heart, the center of imperial power, its money, it's banks. And he would be in the midst of it. His fight was beginning. History was being made. He took a deep breath, aware of the crazy smell of honeysuckle that masked the small wooden shed bordering the patio, their armory, their weapons cache, and now the hiding place of C4 plastic explosive that he'd heard smelled like almonds. Almonds and honeysuckle. He glanced at Tracy. How crazy does it get. Was this really happening? Was he crazy, too?

The same evening, soon after Michael pedaled home from work at SRI, Angela called. She asked him to contact Kim again. "We haven't heard from him in over a month, and with the strike and the university being in turmoil again. . ." Angela' s voice was thick with worry. "I wasn't able to get him on the phone—it was no longer in service."

Michael laughed. "Maybe Tracy didn't pay the bill!"

"Well, I don't know what's happened. Please find him and tell him there's a stack of mail here for him, some from the university. And let us know if he's OK. He's been in such a strange mood, and that girl he's with—well. . . and here in Berkeley the police are all over the place, gas masks hanging on their belts. . ."

"OK, Mom, I'll ride over to Tracy's right away. He'll be OK. Don't worry. I don't imagine he'll want to tangle with the police again."

Michael dragged his bike from the garage where he'd left it a few minutes earlier. His street was blocked to cars by the police, and he'd been riding to work on his bike. Tracy's house was only a few blocks farther. As he pedaled along the street in front of the Professor's house, he could hear music and voices blaring from the loudspeakers in front of the Old Union, the HQ of the strike committee. Students were gathered in clumps on fraternity house lawns and dorm steps. They would be asking each other about what would happen now. Was the semester over? What about finals? Should they go home?

In twenty minutes or so he was knocking at Tracy's door. As he waited he eyed the window next to the door, remembering how the last time he'd been here Tracy had checked to see who had knocked. And sure enough, the curtain pulled back and he caught a glimpse of her face. "Well," she said, smiling as she pulled open the door. "It's brother Michael."

"Is Kim here?" he asked.

"Yeah sure. He's in the kitchen. Come on in"

After turning the dead bolts on the front door, she led him into the house and called out sharply, "It's Michael here to see you."

When Michael entered the kitchen, he saw Kim rolling up a large piece of paper, that looked like an architectural drawing of a building. "So, Michael, what's up?" Kim said jamming the paper awkwardly into a kitchen drawer. "It's been a while. How's it going?"

He shrugged, watching Kim struggle to shut the drawer. "It's kind of crazy on campus, but I guess I'm OK. How about you?"

"Yeah. . ." and he shot a quick glance at Tracy, as if asking for help.

"Kim," Tracy said, "why don't we make some tea."

"OK, sure," and he grabbed the kettle and filled it while Tracy reached for tea and cups from a cabinet.

"Mom's worried about you, Kim. She says your phone is disconnected or something and there's a stack of mail—some of it from the university."

"Yeah, well, we're tired of contributing to capitalist AT&T for a while. And God knows what the university wants." He pulled out a chair from the table. "Come on, Michael. Sit down. He set out the cups and saucers while Tracy spooned tea into the teapot, and when the kettle boiled, poured it onto the tea and then their cups. She picked up one of the steaming teacups, then scooped up the newspaper lying on the counter. "I'll leave you two and catch up on the latest treacheries," and she opened the door to the patio and closed it firmly behind her.

Michael settled at the table and surveyed the room. At one end the counters were covered with drawing materials, pencils, rulers of varied shapes, papers. He knew Kim was working part time for an architect and was relieved to see evidence of it. He wasn't just doing stuff for his leftist group.

Kim sat across from him, leaned his chair on its back legs and sipped his tea. He then shot Michael a sly smile. "So how's the work at SRI these days? Defense Department happy with it?"

Michael sipped his tea. Kim was needling him. Did he want to begin that conversation? He gave Kim a long, studied look. "Work's fine. Interesting."

"But you're funded by DOD."

"Right." he said quickly, simply. "And how's your work going?" He pointed to the drawing materials on the counter.

Kim snorted. "It's come to a halt. Berkeley's in chaos. Both students and faculty think they're accomplishing something. But what!"

Michael gave Kim another long look. At least they agreed on that point. "I ask the same question," he said, quietly.

"But, Michael, you're just being passive, doing absolutely nothing, actually working for the fucking government. How can you live with yourself?"

Michael took a deep breath. He didn't want to fight with Kim. That wasn't why he was here. "Kim, Mom wants to know you're OK. Are you OK?"

"Sure!"

"And are you still involved with that radical group of Tracy's?"

"I see them sometimes. They believe they can make real changes, get rid of the stupid tyrants who wield power over the world. Instead give power to the people—workers, students, whites, blacks, people of color."

Michael sighed and rose from the table. "Well, I've got to go. It's getting late. The police get edgy in my neighborhood when it gets dark." He moved toward the front door, Kim trailing behind him.

Kim grinned. "Yeah, those pigs can get nervous." Michael had his hand on the doorknob when Kim blurted, "so Michael, are you still seeing Gina? How is she?"

"She's OK. Upset with the situation, of course. I'll be seeing her this weekend, going to drive her up to her parents in Napa. As you know, the campus is impossible right now." He opened the door, locked eyes with Kim, and said quietly, "see you, brother. Take it easy, OK? And call Mom."

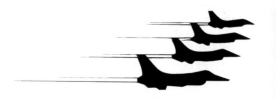

Chapter Twenty-Four

S tanford, June, 1970; It was well after midnight when Michael took the exit off the bay bridge and swerved onto highway 280 heading south. It had been a good day—a busy day, but he'd felt a certain euphoria being with Gina all day, working together, helping her move her belongings, her books and clothes to her family's house in the vineyard. He laughed to himself. Imagine being happy about lugging boxes down two flights of stairs and then carrying them up again to her room at her parents'. He hummed along with the tune playing on his car radio, a Judy Collins song. Gina's family had been welcoming, even her father, who sometimes gave the impression he suspected Michael had dishonorable intentions concerning his daughter. Michael grinned. And he did, of course, if that phrase meant he wanted to sleep with her. If it meant he didn't intend to marry her, Olivetti was wrong. He can't imagine living without her. He hadn't asked her yet, but he would soon.

Suddenly, he realized the music had stopped and the announcer was stating that a news report had just been received of a bombing at the Bank of America in Belmont. Startled, Michael turned up the volume and listened carefully to the announcer's words. He knew that Belmont was a few miles north of Palo Alto. He'd be driving by there soon. *No people were killed or injured in the blast,* he said, *but considerable damage was done to the building. Police report they don't know who is responsible for the bombing. They suspect that one of the local revolutionary organizations set the bomb.*

At hearing the announcer's words he caught his breath. He drove the rest of the way home trying to remember what he knew about that organization that Tracy belonged to, RU, the Revolutionary Union. Could it be the one responsible for the bombing? Could Kim possibly be mixed up in this shit? Michael felt a queasy feeling in his gut, a kind of foreboding. He remembered the sheet of paper with the building plan that Kim had jammed so furtively into Tracy's kitchen drawer. Then he thought of the other bombings he'd heard of—like the one last week after Nixon's speech, when during the Stanford ROTC protest, the Behavior Science building burst into flames. And there were those Weather Underground bank bombings in Chicago, and the one in New York where the guy who set the bomb blew himself up.

He sighed and switched off his radio, continuing toward home. Would life ever get back to normal? It was true that the streets near is house were now quieter and the police were no longer constantly around, but what would be blown up next? He parked his car, dragged himself up the stairs to his apartment, collapsed into bed and tried to fall asleep. He hadn't been in bed long before he was awakened by the sound of the doorbell ringing and found a wild-eyed, disheveled Kim standing on his doorstep.

Kim was sweating in spite of the cool night air, and his fingers trembled as he continued to push the doorbell, which he could hear ringing inside. Exhausted, his breath came in gasps. He'd parked his car six blocks away, in front of the house Michael used to live in and had walked at a steady pace to get here, trying to fight his panic, hoping to appear calm and normal, as if he were a student going back to his dorm. When he reached Michael's he'd raced up the stairs in a frenzy to reach safety. Now he rang the bell again. After what seemed like a century he heard footsteps padding across the floor inside the apartment. The door was opened by barefooted Michael dressed in shorts and T shirt, his hair drooping over his eyes. "Kim! What the hell!" and he stood in the doorway, rock-like, gaping at him.

"Michael, I need a place to crash! Sorry I woke you up, but . ." He'd been rehearsing in his mind what he'd say to Michael, what fucking story he'd tell, but the words just didn't come.

Still staring, Michael moved away from the door and with a flick of his head indicated for him to go in. "For Christ sake, what's happened? It's the middle of the night!"

"Yeah, I know, but, you see, Tracy. . ." He fumbled a moment, trying desperately to remember what story he'd made up on the way here to tell him. "We had a fight, a big fight—and Tracy threw me out and I had nowhere else to go."

Michael tossed him a look, a kind of wary look, like he didn't believe the Tracy story and suspected something worse. "Shit, Kim!" Michael turned away from him, and holding his hand on his head as if he had a serious headache, said slowly, "I really don't know what you're up to, but I guess you can sleep on the couch." He grabbed a blanket from a shelf in the closet next to his bed and tossed It to him. "The bathroom is over there," and he pointed to the open door behind him. "We can talk later after we've had some sleep. I'm fucking going back to bed!" He switched off the light on the table next to the bed, leaving the room lit only by light from the open bathroom.

Kim collapsed into a drugged-like sleep, and when he opened his eyes he found the room filled with light. He quickly closed them again and yanked the blanket up over his head. It took a moment to remember where he was. He was on Michael's couch, of course, and now, when he shifted the blanket from his face, he saw that Michael, sprawled on a leather chair, held a newspaper up before him. Fuck. Kim suppressed a groan and turned over to face the back of the couch. What would he tell Michael? Had he believed the Tracy story? He clamped his jaw tight. He would say nothing about what he'd done. But what was the next step? Did he actually need to run? Nobody had seen him there. He'd been half a block away when he heard the bomb explode. He'd been walking briskly through the parking lot to the residential street beyond the shopping mall. He'd watched Kevin place the device and set the timer. Then they both slipped away—in opposite directions. When he heard the shock of the explosion he felt a moment of elation, of pride. The device had worked and he was certain the area was unoccupied. He turned back to watch the smoldering flames and smoke. Was he truly certain the night watchman had left the bank for his rounds at the other buildings? Then he heard the sirens screaming, lots of them, and knew he had to get away fast, but keep cool. He walked rapidly to his car and drove off at a decorous speed, his eyes checking the rear-view mirror, watching for tails. He took a circuitous route to make sure he wasn't being followed. When he finally reached Princeton Road and eyed Tracy's house, he was breathing almost normally—until wham, like a blow to his head, he knew he couldn't go there. What had he been thinking? The FBI could be watching the house at this very moment. They knew about the guns in the shed. They probably had files on anyone who frequented the house—certainly he and Tracy. How could he have made such a stupid mistake?

Now as he lay on Michael's couch, his knees drawn up to his chest, his face pressed against the rough upholstery, he wanted to scream. What would happen now? What had he done? Why had he agreed to do it! Like a little kid he'd thought he was punishing the bullies for beating him up. Payback! Who was he kidding? Had he just wanted to be admired by Tracy? By the real revolutionaries? Was he trying to show Gina how tough he was, how brave? Was he that unsure of himself? He'd been playing with fire, like a dumb kid, like an actor in a movie, playing a role, a revolutionary, a fucking Maoist?

He groaned. The Mao doctrine was just a load of shit. He'd always known that. Mao was no holier than Stalin. And he'd known that the police had checked out Tracy's house for weapons permits, and most likely had informed the FBI. Why else did everyone coming to the house check around themselves for watchers? Why hadn't he planned to go somewhere else after the bombing instead of Tracy's? Had the knock on his head made him so very stupid? And there were his parents—and Michael. How could he face them? He, the bomber, the Maoist revolutionary. That thought forced him to sit up, throw the blanket to the floor, and take a deep breath. Michael was staring at him.

Michael, who sat on his one upholstered chair opposite the couch had been watching Kim thrash about on it, the blanket clutched over his face—for for what seemed like hours. The San Francisco Chronicle he'd been reading had slid to the floor. He'd read the piece about the bombing of the Bank of America building again and again. The FBI was investigating, it said, *but the agent in charge could not comment on what organization or individual they suspected had set the bomb. The device had exploded at 11:03 Saturday night. There were no casualties, but the building was seriously damaged. The phrase POWER TO THE PEOPLE was spray-painted on a remaining wall of the building, suggesting that one of the local revolutionary organizations such as the Black Panthers, Venceremos, Revolutionary Union, or the Red Guard was the perpetrator. The agent assured the public that during the last months the FBI had been investigating all of these organizations, and as the forensic evidence at the bombing site was analyzed, the criminals involved would be identified.*

When Michael first read the words *Revolutionary Union* he'd felt an explosion in his head. Now he was certain Kim was involved. Last night he'd strongly suspected, but hadn't allow himself to believe Kim could be so stupid. His eyes now fastened on his blanketed body twisting and turning on the couch. He thought of the white frayed look on Kim's face when he stood at his door last night around 1 A.M. He'd stumbled over his words, he'd been inarticulate, wild-eyed, like a scared child When had that bomb gone off? He glanced again at the newspaper. 11:03 PM. Time enough. Holy Shit! It was really possible! A sick feeling swirled in his gut.

Now the blanket suddenly flew from Kim's shrouded form onto the floor. He sat up, his hair in dank tangles, his eyes shadowed, the skin on his gaunt face slick with sweat. "What are you staring at, Michael?" Kim croaked, glaring at him.

Michael hesitated a beat before answering. "I'm staring at you, brother. Trying to make sense out of all this shit." He made a sweeping gesture that included Kim on the couch and the newspaper on the floor.

"Yeah?" He evaded Michael's look and glanced down at the newspaper, his hair hanging over his eyes.

Michael leaned forward and picked up the paper. "Yeah, I'm trying to put pieces of a puzzle together—like why you're here, why your story about Tracy's throwing you out doesn't compute—and what I'm reading here scares the shit out of me," and he tapped at the paper he held in his hand.

Kim straightened his back against the couch and wiped the sweat off his forehead with the back of his hand. "I told you already. Tracy and I split up."

Dropping the paper on the table next to him, Michael moved to his small kitchen area, and tossing a quick glance over his shoulder, said, "and why don't I believe you?"

Kim shrugged. "Beats me!" and he bent over to put on his shoes he'd taken off before he'd taken refuge under the blanket.

As Michael filled the kettle with water, intending to make instant coffee, he eyed Kim as he tied his shoes, noting how his fingers shook as they fumbled with his shoelaces. Suddenly, still bent forward, Kim lowered his head into his hands and moaned, a plaintive, haunted sound. Michael froze. He turned off the water, and still holding the kettle in his hand, stared at his brother. Shit! With a sharp intake of breath he set the kettle in the sink and moved slowly toward Kim, who lifted his head from his hands and gave him a frantic look. "I'm in deep trouble, Michael, and I don't know what to do—or where to go. I'm scared. I'm fucked!"

Clamping his lips together, he sat next to Kim on the couch, wondering if he should keep his mouth shut, wait for Kim to talk—like a shrink would do? If Kim were really involved in this bank bombing, he was truly fucked, big time. And was it something he wanted to hear? This was serious stuff. He felt a wall of caution build around his heart. He spoke slowly, carefully. "So why are you scared, Kim? What's happened?"

Kim pushed himself up from the couch and stumbled toward the sunlit window overlooking the street. "What hasn't happened? For one thing the FBI is probably on to me."

"The FBI?" He waited for Kim to say more. Did he really want him to?

After a long pause, Kim turned from the window and gave him a long, questioning look. Was he wondering if his brother could be trusted? He moved to the table where Michael had left the newspaper and picked it up. Rapidly skimming the page, he then tossed it back onto the floor in an angry gesture. He turned and faced Michael. "FBI guys could have been watching Tracy's house. It's possible they saw me drive by at midnight."

"At midnight?" Again, he waited for him to continue.

"Yeah, as you seem to have guessed, I was there. At the bombing."

Michael's gut clamped. Did he want to hear this? Did he want to get involved? "Shit, Kim, I didn't want to believe it! How could you be so stupid!! Did they force you to be there? Those revolutionary idiot friends of yours. . .like Tracy?"

"No." He took in a deep breath. "I did it willingly. Sort of. I wanted to make my mark, do something big, important. For the cause."

"Jesus, Kim! For Mao? For the revolution?"

Kim gave a violent shake of his head. "Not for fucking Mao, for Christ sake." He collapsed on the couch and put his head in his hands again. "I don't know why I went along with it. You're right. I was stupid, an idiot. But I did want to change the world, stop the war, bring peace." He pounded his knees with his fists and jumped up, rushing again to the window. "But who am I kidding? I was in a rage. I wanted revenge. I kept remembering how it felt to lie helpless on the cold bare asphalt while the pigs taunted and humiliated us. Last year at Santa Rita jail."

Michael moved toward him and touched his shoulder. A surge of sympathy was dislodging the wall around his heart. Kim was his brother, part of his life. Maybe he could find some way to help him. "OK, Kim, why don't you tell me exactly what you did there at the bombing—and who was with you."

"I can't name names. Someone else made the bomb and planted it, but I was watching, making sure there were no people around, watching for cops or witnesses, that the bank would be empty when it was blown."

Michael listened to his description of what he'd been ordered to do by his collective leader, how he'd done the surveillance of the building and it's surroundings, how the night of the bombing he'd made sure the building was empty, the night guard had gone on his rounds of the mall, and finally, the bomb go off and had cautiously fled the scene. Then he'd panicked when he thought of the FBI watching Tracy's house and recognizing his car. Suddenly, Michael's chest constricted. Tracy's car! Was it parked outside on the street in front of this house? He turned to Kim, who was slumped on the couch, a blank expression on his face. "Kim, where did you leave the car?"

Kim gave him an anguished look. "I told you I panicked. I forgot you had moved. I parked it in front of Julies—then walked here from there."

"Julies? Shit, Kim, did anyone see you?"

"I don't know. I don't think so. I tried to act normal, but I was so scared."

Michael stared at him. So what would happen now? Should Kim turn himself in? Was there any way he could be helped to get out of this mess? Could Kim avoid being caught? And did he want to help him, taking on the risk of being considered an accessory after the fact? He had to think. This was serious stuff. His life, career, his future was at stake. But then. . .Kim was his brother. Helping him was the right thing to do.

Chapter Twenty-Five

Berkeley, June, 1970; Carrying a cup of Sunday morning coffee in his hand, Hank was heading for his study when the phone rang. Glancing around for Angela, who he remembered had gone into the garden, he set down his cup and picked up the phone. It was Michael, who gave him a brief, garbled greeting and then plunged into a shrill jumble of words Hank could barely decipher. "Wait, Michael, hold on! Slow down!"

Speaking more slowly, but unsteadily, Michael said, "Dad, we're leaving right away. We're coming home. Kim's with me. We need to talk to you. OK?"

He was startled by the ominous tone in Michael's voice. "Sure, Michael. But what's happened?"

"We'll tell you when we get there. Bye, Dad," and he hung up.

Hank slowly set the phone onto the receiver and stared down at it. Whatever Michael wanted to tell him, it wasn't good. He'd sounded so tense, so tightly wound up. Was it about Kim? Was he sick? Into some serious trouble? He felt as if something were pressing against his rib cage. He took a deep breath and went out the door to find Angela.

Less than an hour later when he heard Michael's car on the driveway, Angela and he were outside on the deck in the morning sunshine. While they'd waited, Hank had found himself unable to sit still in his heavy redwood chair, and kept jumping up every time he heard a car driving up their hillside road. Angela, too, had been unable to relax. She'd hopped up again and again—to fix coffee, she'd say or something to eat. Now they both were standing at the top of deck stairs their eyes fastened on the car doors opening in the driveway below. Angus was dancing around the car yelping joyously, as the two men emerged.

Michael waved to them as he climbed out of the car, a wooden smile on his face. Then Kim unfolded himself and peered up at them. "Hi," he said quietly. Hank noted how his thin form was slow to straighten up and how his face seemed do have narrowed. And his eyes. . . they stared straight ahead, blankly, a flat, stone gray shadowed by black. Kim glanced briefly at Angus, mumbled something to the dog, and reached for the stair railing. He seemed to slink up the stairs, looking rather like Angus when he'd been disobedient. He glanced at Angela, noting her strained face, her troubled eyes. He watched as she stepped forward, stretching her arms to Kim as he reached the top of the stairs. "Kim, are you OK? Are you sick? Has something happened?"

Kim allowed her to hold him a moment, dropping his head down onto her shoulder, his russet-tinged hair stringy and unkempt. "No, Mom, I'm just kind of burnt-out."

Michael stepped up behind him and shot Hank a sharp look. Clapping him on the shoulder, Hank eyed Michael's tightly closed mouth, the shadowed eyes, causing a sick feeling in his gut. "So what's all this? Tell us, for Christ sake! What's going on?"

"Dad, we need to talk." He strode onto the deck, shoved his hands into his pockets, glanced back at Kim, who hadn't moved from the top of the stairs, Angela still holding his arm.

A spurt of anger, of frustration shot up Hank's spine. "By all means. Talk!" He pointed to the wooden chairs around the table, kicking at one of them!"

Angela broke away from Kim, tossing Hank a warning look, but smiling, first at Kim then Michael. "Would you like something? Have you had breakfast?"

"We're OK, Mom," Michael said, and he pulled out a chair, glancing at Kim, indicating wordlessly for him to sit down. When Kim had taken his seat, Michael took the one opposite. Hank and Angela joined them, taking the other two chairs on either side of their sons, their eyes sweeping from one to the other. Michael spoke first, avoiding eye contact, controlling his voice. "Did either of you read this morning's paper?'

"Only the headlines about the bombings, ROTC bombings at Stanford, Weather Underground bombings in Chicago, and one on the peninsula. So. . ?" Where was that bombing on the peninsula? Belmont, was it. . .near where Kim was living? He glanced at Angela who was staring at Michael.

"Was there something we should have read?" she asked, "something we should know?"

Michael then cast his eyes at Kim, who evaded his. He took a deep breath as if he were diving into a rushing river. "Yeah." he said quietly. "You should have read the story about the Bank of America bombing in Belmont, allegedly placed by one of the local radical organizations just before midnight last night. The Revolutionary Union was named as one of them."

Hank's heart jumped. That was the radical group that Kim's girl Tracy hung out with. Angela let out a small cry, her eyes wide with alarm. "And...?" Hank said, finally.

Kim then lifted his head, which had been bent forward as if he were studying the redwood planks of the table. He gave Hank a direct look, then fastened his eyes on Angela. His voice was hoarse. "And I was there. My Revolutionary Union collective planned the bombing and I was one of three who took part. I did the surveillance."

Hank felt as though the oxygen had been sucked from his lungs. "Jesus Christ!" he murmured under his breath. How could Kim have been so stupid! Had he really fallen for all that Mao shit!

Angela's hands flew to her face. Her eyes filled with tears. "Oh, Kim, how could you do such a thing! Was anyone hurt, killed?"

"No, Mom. Nobody was hurt or killed. That was my job—to make sure that didn't happen. And I didn't build the bomb—or plant it. Another guy did that." His eyes were desperate against his white face.

Angela reached for his hand, which clutched the edge of the table. "And was that girl there with you—that Tracy?"

166

"No, Mom. She wasn't needed then. She'd helped with the surveillance earlier in the week, but she stayed home."

A surge of rage suddenly catapulted Hank to his feet. He needed to move, explode. He suppressed the urge to roar like Lear, pacing the boards underfoot, and clung to the back of his chair for support. "Kim," he said, forcing his voice to stay under control, "Were there witnesses? Were you seen?"

Kim let out a sharp breath. "As far as I know there were no witnesses."

"And afterwords, your escape plan?"

Kim hesitated. "Well," he stuttered, "I drove the car slowly, and headed for Tracy's. When I got there it hit me that the police knew about the guns that were stored there—that they'd checked them for licenses. . ."

Hank froze. He couldn't believe what he was hearing. "There were guns in the house? You were going home to a house filled with guns the police knew about! In your own car! Shit, Kim, what the hell were you thinking of when you moved into that house—and what kind of outfit is this RU? Didn't they plan? Jesus, even a low-level thief would have a get-away plan."

"Yeah, I guess we didn't think about that."

Hank clapped his hands over his head, pacing the deck. "A fucking bunch of amateurs! What did you think you were playing at? How could you have been so stupid!"

Angela moved toward Hank and gave him another warning look. "Hank, they're just students, barely twenty-one!"

Hank glared at her, thinking that when he jumped into enemy territory during the war he was only nineteen. He stared at Kim. "So what did you do when you got to Tracy's?"

"I guess I panicked. When I remembered the FBI could be watching the house I rushed to Michael's—except then I remembered he'd moved."

Hank felt his blood pressure rising, his heart pounding. He forced himself to calm down. He tried to slow his breathing. These kids had no training unlike he'd had to go through. Angela was right.

They were children playing at grown-up games. He shot a wary look at Kim, afraid to ask his next question. "And where did you leave the car?"

"In front of the place Michael used to live. Then I walked as cautiously as I could to where he is now."

Hank then turned to Michael, attempting to steady his breathing. "And Michael, did you know that that Kim was living in a house where guns were stored and didn't tell us?"

Michael bit his lip. "Yeah. I couldn't tell you. It would have been a betrayal to Kim. And you and Mom would have gone out of your mind." With a quick gesture he smoothed back his hair, glancing briefly at Kim. "We don't tell you guys everything we do, you know." He then turned back to Hank, giving him a direct look. "Tracy was a close friend of my housemate, Julie. You knew about Julie. I told you she was radical, a member of Revolutionary Union, and that was the main reason I moved. You knew that, but not that when her friend, Tracy, also a RU member was at the house, she told me about the weapons stored there. Kim knew, too."

Hank stared at Michael. Then at Kim, a wave of helplessness washing over him. Kim was in serious trouble.

Michael rose from his chair, fixing Hank with an unflinching look. "And, Dad, I persuaded Kim to come here for advice. For us to help him decide what to do. IF there's something he can do to get out of this mess. I told him that you of all people would stand by his side. In spite of the possible legal consequences. You're his parents. You love him. As I do."

"We do love him, and I want to help him, of course. He's our son."

Michael turned to Kim. "But Kim, I think you now need to explain to Dad how you feel about your radical behavior. How you've changed, how mistaken you were. Tell them, please, Kim. . .like you told me. OK?"

Hank listened to Kim's emotional confession, wanting to believe him, feeling a certain relief, but after having heard Kim's description of the bombing, of how he'd been driving the car that Tracy had loaned him and left it on the street, he felt a deepening fog of uncertainty. What should Kim do now? What should they do? They must think carefully, calmly. The thought of Kim's being arrested, interrogated, sentenced to prison was horrifying. Should the boy flee, leave the country, become a fugitive? Or hire a good lawyer and turn himself in? That might be the sensible thing to do—certainly for Angela, Michael and himself, considering the serious trouble they'd be in, if by helping Kim to avoid arrest they would be labeled by the authorities as complicit, accessories after the fact.

But no! His eyes fixed on Kim, then Angela and Michael. He clenched his fist. He shot Kim a look of determination. "Kim, we have work to do. We'll need to discuss this from every angle. You must try to remember the details of your involvement—both with RU and the bombing itself—the planning, surveillance, bomb placement and escape. We might be able to help you to evade arrest and conviction, but we need to put all the information you can come up with under the microscope. OK, let's get to work."

A few hours later, Michael was on the Bay bridge again. He looked out at the wisps of fog that clung to the tops of city buildings across the bay, thinking about how violent protests had sprung up from coast to coast since the Cambodian incursion. FBI agents were being kept busy these days, locally too. There'd been the explosion at the Behavioral Science building during the ROTC protest last week—and they were still trying to find out who had bombed the San Francisco police station in February, four months ago. Maybe it's not so easy for the FBI to find out who was responsible. And maybe these events would reduce attention to the Belmont bombing. And something else. Isn't it possible that Tracy's house was not being watched the night of the bombing around midnight? And Kim was not spotted? FBI agents and informers had their hands full.

As Michael drove automatically through the Sunday morning bridge traffic, he kept replaying the scene that occurred that morning on his parents' deck. While birds chirped among the red leaves of the plum tree overhanging the deck railing and the sun warmed their backs, they plotted how to get Kim out of the hole he'd dug for himself. The image of Kim's gaunt face flashed before him. As they talked he'd looked as if he were unraveling, as if he needed cave to hide in. Michael even wondered if he were having a nervous breakdown.

Kim had agreed to the suggestion that he unobtrusively move back into his old room in the guest house. Hank figured this could be a prudent first move. Then they'd wait to see what happened when the bombing was investigated. He'd also agreed to break off with Tracy, which he said he was quite willing to do. In fact, he'd said he'd been wanting to split up with her for weeks, but hadn't known how to do it.

After considerable discussion it was then decided that Michael should go to Tracy's to pick up Kim's belongings. A group decision, of course, Michael thought wryly. Furthermore, the four of them composed the brief but apologetic letter that Michael would take to Tracy, supposedly from Kim, to break off their relationship and move out and to allow Michael to "pick up his stuff, especially his architecture tools." Kim then added his own bit about how they'd had good times, but he wasn't the guy for her, and that if anyone asked about him, to tell them he needed to concentrate on school. His grades were suffering. He'd been running around too much. He was exhausted and needed time to find his "center."

They'd decided he shouldn't mention Kim's work with RU. Hank had said that if the FBI got hold of the note—or if Tracy were questioned, Kim shouldn't present them with his hand-written evidence of his involvement in the organization. Hank had also warned Michael to be cautious but casual when he approached Tracy's house. He should act as if it were a normal favor he was doing his brother by picking up his things, helping him move back home. He should remain alert, of course, checking out the terrain, so to speak. Michael smiled, thinking how Hank had been drawing on his old OSS training as he'd lectured him, advising him to memorize the cover story, at least the one they'd settled on so far.

Now Michael had reached Tracy's neighborhood. When he turned the corner onto Princeton, he scrutinized the street ahead of him. Cars were parked in driveways, and across the street from Tracy's he noted a woman sweeping the cement path in front of the house. He felt a sense of relief when she turned and went inside. She was just a neighbor, and not an FBI informer? He parked in front of Tracy's, and climbing out of his car he reached for a rucksack, which he slung over his shoulder. He wore jeans and a T shirt and hoped, if he were being watched, he looked like any other grad student. As he approached Tracy's house he noticed her shiny new Datsun parked in the carport and figured she was home. It was the one she drove after lending her old VW to Kim. He felt in his pocket for Kim's letter, and straightened his shoulders. He wasn't looking forward to this meeting. He must stay cool, calm and casually friendly, but watch his tongue. On no account must she suspect he knows about Kim's connection to the bombing—or to RU. He was here merely to collect his kid brother's stuff, that Kim was not feeling well and had gone home.

He walked briskly up the path and rang the doorbell. After a minute or two, the curtain in the window next to the door twitched aside and Tracy opened the door. She peered at him with a questioning look, then stepped back, indicating for him to enter. "So if it isn't Michael. What can I do for you?"

He scanned the room and listened for voices but he didn't hear anyone else in the house and assumed she was alone. He explained his mission, that Kim had come to him, then moved home and he needed to collect Kim's belongings. "And he said to tell you he left the blue VW in front of Julie's, where I used to live. The keys are inside."

She fixed her wide blue eyes on his, and after a pause, as if taking it all in, said, with a touch of surprise, "Julie's?"

"Yeah, he told me you two had a. . . well, a disagreement. He was exhausted and confused and had forgotten I'd moved six blocks away onto the campus." He then handed her the letter. She held it in her hand, still gazing at him—then abruptly pointed to the kitchen.

"OK. His school stuff is in the back of the kitchen. On the table by the window. Help yourself. His clothes and things are in the second bedroom down the hall."

He nodded, and watching her briefly as she slit open the envelope, he went into the kitchen and began collecting Kim's papers and tools and packing them into his rucksack and a large plastic bag he'd brought along. When he returned to the living room Tracy was sitting on the couch, holding the letter in her hand. "Tracy," he said, "I'll get his other stuff, OK?" She turned, gave him a rather absent look and nodded.

It took only a few minutes to dig up Kim's scattered clothes and toilet articles. He stuffed them into the bags and went back to the living room, finding Tracy still sitting and holding the open letter. "OK, I think I have everything." he said. "I guess I'll take off." He eyed the front door, anxious to get out of there, but wanting to be polite. He paused and looked at her more closely. She didn't seem upset or hurt. Puzzled, perhaps. He pointed to the letter. "I hope you're OK. Kim told me what he was going to say. He's really exhausted, Tracy. He needs time to recover, to rest."

She shrugged. "I'm fine, Michael. I think we were both getting kind of tired of each other. Life goes on." Tossing him a wide smile, she said, "tell him I hope he feels better," and after a pause, she said quietly, "and tell him to keep his head down." She waved and he shouldered the bags and went out the door.

While moving toward his car he feigned a casualness he did not feel. Dad's instructions to behave like a normal guy helping someone move echoed in his ear. He piled Kim's belongings onto the back seat of the car, noting as he did so that the street was quiet, except for a mocking bird's piercing call. He drove away without incident and when he reached the highway he realized he could breathe normally. By the time he arrived back in Berkeley, his pulse had quieted and he truly turned into the person he'd been pretending to be—the one who helped his brother.

That evening, about eleven o'clock, on his way home from his long, troubled day with Kim and his family, he swung by Julie's house. He wanted to know if Tracy had come for the car, but there it was, parked just as Kim had told him. Would she have conferred with her accomplices? Ask them for help, advice? Had they suggested she leave it where it was? How long would it be before the police decided to take a closer look at the blue VW. Police cars patrolled campus streets constantly since the violent protests and the ROTC bombing, and Kim's finger prints would be all over the car. Surely, Tracy's collective members would advise her to fetch the car as soon as possible. Taking a sharp intake of breath, Michael drove around the block and headed for home. He was exhausted. He couldn't think anymore. All he wanted was sleep.

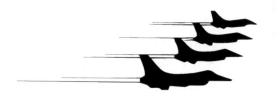

Chapter Twenty-Six

Berkeley, June, 1970; Kim, his hands under the running water at his bathroom sink, stared at his image in the mirror. A week had passed since he moved back into his parents' guest house, and the circles under his eyes had faded somewhat. For the last two nights he'd not been awakened by terrifying nightmares. His fears of immediate arrest had quieted, although his heart raced each time the phone rang—and when he drove to work his hands were slick with sweat as they gripped the steering wheel watching for police cars. Now he poured more liquid soap over his hands, attempting to remove the stubborn traces of oil. He'd been working on his old car that morning, the one with the porcupine still painted on its hood, trying to get it back in shape, so that he wouldn't need to borrow Mom's Volvo to get to work.

He'd heard almost nothing about the car he'd abandoned when he'd fled to Michael for refuge. Michael had called last Tuesday and said the blue VW was no longer parked at Julie's. He'd driven by Tracy's house, he'd said, but it wasn't parked there either, so he didn't know if she had come for her car or not. Maybe she'd hidden it somewhere. Or maybe the police had picked it up. It had been registered in Tracy's name, and unless she'd reported it missing, which he doubted she'd do, the police wouldn't investigate it's ownership until its abandonment was reported or noticed by the police. Maybe someone else reported it. Then Kim stared at himself in the mirror. Maybe someone stole it. That was a startling thought! He'd left the keys in the ignition, so someone might have. What would happen then? He shook his head and looked down at the oily water. Whenever he thought of that car he felt like he'd been caught in its gears, mangled and trapped.

He resumed scrubbing the oil on his skin and forced himself to stop obsessing about Tracy's car. Instead he thought about his job with the architect office in Oakland where he'd been drawing thin lines on tracing paper and checking blueprints. His bosses had stopped sending him to building sites over a month ago, and what a relief that had been. He'd failed dismally at recruiting the construction workers to join the revolution, which his collective expected him to do. Thank God that was over. The guys who worked for Newman were happy with their work. They were well paid and well treated by their supervisors. He'd never known quite how to explain their views to his collective. Tracy said he just didn't try hard enough to convince them they were wrong, which happened to be true. He'd been a half-hearted revolutionary, after all, and it was a relief to be through with it.

He shook off the water from his hands and inspected them before reaching for one of Mom's clean towels. He gave himself another glance in the mirror as he dried his hands. Did his stupidity show on his face? He couldn't stop being furious with himself. As Michael said, how would he get out of this hole he'd dug for himself? He fucking didn't know!

Moving to the dresser next to his bed he lifted his comb, but before he'd started to deal with his shaggy hair, he noticed a brown bobby pin stuck in a crack at the back of the dresser. It must be one of Gina's she'd left here before they split up. He never brought Tracy here, and anyway, she was blonde and would just shove her long hair behind her ears or clip it with a rubber band. Had Gina stayed here with Michael? That thought gave him an uncomfortable feeling. He couldn't be jealous, could he? His relationship with her was quite over, ended, but it might be awkward to have her as a sister-in-law instead of a lover. He shook off that thought and flung down the comb. He had enough to worry about. Like Tracy's car.

His feet felt heavy as he climbed the stairs for Sunday lunch with his parents. Was it only a week since Michael brought him here—so reluctantly on his own part—to confess his crime to his parents, his idiocy, and ask them for advice? Michael had been adamant, insisting that they would have his best interests at heart, and he'd been right, except it had been painful, humiliating, to face them, expecting Dad's rage, his disgust, his disappointment. How much he had wanted his parents approval.

Now he'd opened the back door and caught the good smell of a roast cooking in the oven. He smiled to himself. Mom had been feeding him well, since he was home. In spite of everything, both she and Dad had been wonderful. They wanted to help him and they weren't sure how. He'd put them in a perilous quandary, which caused him more shame and guilt. He really ought to just cut and run—to Canada or Mexico. The sound of Mom's voice from the kitchen and the smell of roasting meat stopped his brooding. His stomach told him he was actually hungry.

Angela was smiling at him as he moved quickly into the kitchen. "So Kim, did you get your car working?"

"I'm not sure. It sounds better, but I can't tell until I drive it up the hill. I cleaned the points and checked the carburetor, but it may need new spark plugs."

"Maybe you should take it to Andy's, that garage Hank swears by."

Kim could hear the TV from the next room, "Yeah, maybe. . ." and he gestured to the living room. "Any news?"

He could tell by the shadow that crossed Angela's face that she knew he was referring to his own situation—if the FBI had uncovered anything new about the bombing—or about RU. "Not really," she said, "but Hank's in there watching the news right now."

He nodded and walked into the living room, his eyes on the TV screen. He stopped and stared. Camouflaged American soldiers were shown slogging along a muddy trail through a thick forest of broad-leafed trees and sinuous vines. A helicopter juddered overhead. Vietnam, of course, brought into American living rooms. A burst of anger charged through him. Was there absolutely no way to stop this war?

Hank looked up. "They've continued the heavy bombings in the north. Of population centers. I've been sitting here thinking about the villagers I met during the war—with Ho Chi Minh. I feel so sorry for them. They just wanted to be free of the French and Japanese occupation, of being exploited and impoverished. And they believed we'd help them. Instead we're destroying them."

Kim sank onto the upholstered blue couch without speaking, watching the weary, sweaty faces of the soldiers, and thinking about what Dad had just said about the Vietnamese villagers. Hank's view of the colonist's exploitation of the countries they occupied was not so far from what he'd heard spoken by his collective leader. Not the Mao shit and communism, of course.

Now Hank continued. "But nothing new about your bombing or the one at Stanford last week. They're still investigating, they say," and he gave Kim a sharp glance. "We still have to wait for the other shoe to drop."

Kim took in a deep breath. "Yeah! And I've been having nightmares about being in jail, remembering the Blue Meanies. And prison would be a million times worse."

"I keep thinking," Hank said fixing his brown eyes on his, "if we shouldn't hire a good lawyer and consider turning yourself in."

Kim shot him a quick look, "but. . ."

Hank continued. "It's something to consider. He might get you off."

"But then I'd have to snitch on everyone. I couldn't do that, Dad. And there's Tracy. I couldn't do that to her, especially. I'm not that much of a bastard, I hope. No, I'll wait a while longer to see what turns up. Or I'll skip the country."

As he exchanged looks with Hank, he noted the pain in his father's eyes, an arrow of pain that pierced his own chest. How many people must he hurt before he's through with this fucking situation?

Chapter Twenty-Seven

S tanford, August, 1970; As Michael steered his Ford away from the curb in front of his apartment, he noted the Palo Alto police car gliding down the street in front of the house. The Fall semester would begin in two weeks and a few students were settling in already—as was police surveillance. The city police patrolled the streets in cars, and campus cops were on foot around the quad, the student union and other campus buildings. Michael smiled to himself. Everyone knew that young plainclothes cops and FBI agents were ready to infiltrate organizations and protests. Although nationwide protests had quieted during the summer they all expected the tumult would begin again. He took in a deep breath. What a relief it had been to be able hear the song of birds instead of the whine of police sirens. He couldn't really relax, of course. There was Kim to worry about. The FBI still hadn't identified anyone responsible for the bank bombing. Each day as he picked up the newspaper he dreaded the worst. And there was that damned VW of Tracy's Kim was using the night of the bombing. He still didn't know what had happened to it after it disappeared from Julie's.

Now he had reached El Camino. He was on his way to meet Alistair for lunch at Pete's Harbor, a bayside restaurant a few miles north of Stanford. Alistair had just returned from his parents' home in Philadelphia and would be beginning his first year at Stanford Law. Michael hadn't seen Alistair since that wild night in April after Nixon's Cambodia speech, and so much had happened since then—Kim's radical act followed by sticking to a cover story, and his own deepening love for Gina—and his job at SRI, of course, and Englebart's work connecting computers to people everywhere.

As he drove with open windows along the narrow road leading to the small boat harbor, he felt his tension drift away somewhat. The bay lapping at the edges of the road was riffled by a mild wind and reflected the blue sky. It was all so fresh and clean. Soon he saw the rows of moored boats, their masts cleaving the clear air—and the rustic building festooned with nautical line and lifebuoys, with the sign Pete's Harbor Restaurant painted in large black letters on the white wall. He parked his Ford in the lot next to the building and entered the front door, peering at the tables scattered around the room. By the window facing the harbor he spied Alistair looking tanned and fit, dressed in a light blue shirt and white cotton pants. They greeted each other with claps on the back and wide grins. Michael felt truly happy to see Alistair again and told him so.

"Yeah, and it's truly good to be back. I've missed you, Michael."

They sat opposite each other and gave each other appraising looks. "Alistair, you look like you belong on one of those yachts out there. Your clothes, your tan, your clear blue eyes. The last time we met your eyes were red from studying."

"Or the booze or grass," he said, laughing, glancing quickly at the menu and beckoning to the waiter. "Beer OK? They have it on tap here." After the waiter took the order for beer and abalone, Alistair smiled. "I spent the summer re-charging, spending most of my time on our sailboat on Penobscot Bay—at my grandfather's place in Maine." He paused and glanced out the window at the moored boats. "After Kent State and Cambodia I gave up on anti-war marches and moratoriums. It was hopeless. Nothing changed. You either throw in the towel—or start blowing things up—like the Weather Underground—so I quit. I figure I'll become a lawyer, go into politics, maybe, and affect change from within the establishment!"

Michael gave him an approving look. "Sounds good, Alistair. Go for it! I've been thinking along the same lines—not going into politics—that's not my bag—but the work I'm doing now with computers could bring change, I'm sure—connecting people to information. Maybe people will make smarter choices, like voting for you!"

Alistair laughed. "Right on! Sounds interesting. But Michael, you look like you've been holed up at the lab all summer. So what's been happening while I've been gone? Stanford kids still running amok, blowing up buildings?"

"It's been quiet, more or less. The kids went home."

"I read in the Philadelphia paper about the research destroyed at that fire bombing of the Behavioral Science building—the one during the big ROTC protest, when the windows were broken all over campus."

"Yeah, it was a disaster for the people involved. They lost years of research."

"Did they find out who did it?"

"No, not really. Just a week or so ago that there was a report that a witness saw four guys on two motorcycles ride up to the building and throw fire bombs through the windows. One of the men was black, one brown, the other two were white. They don't know who they were—or what group they were with. The Panthers, Venceremos or Revolutionary Union.

"And wasn't there a bombing near here at a shopping mall somewhere? Of a bank?"

Michael picked up his glass of water, spilling some as he drank. He wiped his mouth on his napkin. "Yeah, in Belmont." He scanned the room, hoping the waiter would bring their order soon. His throat felt tight, but he managed to keep his voice steady, casual. "Nobody was killed or injured—and there were no witnesses. It seems to have gone off the radar screen."

Alistair shook his head. "Curious." They were interrupted by the waiter with their their beer and Alistair lifted his. "OK, Peace, brother," he said, grinning. "Maybe it was the Weather Underground, but they're mostly blowing up banks in New York or Chicago—or themselves. I don't imagine they care about Behavioral Science." He set down his mug, then added, "we saw Bernadine Dohrn, the WUO leader, y'know, at the SDS meeting last year. Your brother, Kim, was there. Hanging out with Tracy Collins. So how's he doing? He got in with those RU people, I remember."

Michael felt his heart tweak and took a swig of beer, thinking that he'd been wondering when the subject of Kim would come up. "Yeah, well, he and Tracy broke up. I think he was getting fed up with those RU people—and he was commuting all over the place, living with Tracy in Menlo, going to school in Berkeley, working for an architect firm. He was exhausted. I thought he was about to have a nervous breakdown."

"Wow. So where is he now?"

"Back in Berkeley, living at my parents'. Has a summer job with an architect firm. He's OK now."

"Good." Alistair leaned back in his chair, gazing out at the bay. "You know, I could never figure out what Kim saw in Tracy. He seemed like a smart kid—but Tracy? An airhead, for sure."

Michael decided not to respond, thinking that Tracy was no airhead. A misguided, radical, but smart. Smart enough not to be caught by the FBI. He changed the subject. "So Alistair, are you and Sara still together?"

"Absolutely. We're thinking of getting married. Maybe a year from now, when I'm in my second year at Law school. She'll be graduating then."

"Great, Alistair. Congratulations," and he held up his mug in toast. They clicked mugs and as they did so, the waiter arrived with their orders of abalone and french fries, and they both dug in.

Alistair glanced up briefly. "And Michael, what about you? Are you still with the lovely Gina?"

Michael, with his mouth full of the delicious abalone, nodded, and after swallowing, said, "absolutely! I popped the question and she said yes, but we'll wait until she graduates next spring."

Alistair grinned. "Great news. Imagine. And life goes on. At least if we don't get drafted."

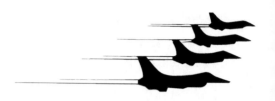

Chapter Twenty-Eight

Berkeley, September, 1970; Kim's shoe laces on one of his sneakers were tangled. As he unwound them, the ringing of the phone caused him to jump and drop the shoe. His heart pounding, he moved slowly to the phone in the corner of his guest house, and with shaking hands, picked up. "Is that you, Bill?" a strangers voice asked. Taking a deep breath, Kim replied that the caller had the wrong number, and he returned to his task, trying to calm himself. Over four months had passed since the bombing, but each time the phone rang he was jolted with a shock of fear, believing it was the police, that the other shoe had dropped.

But maybe he was really getting away with it—or was he kidding himself? A witness could turn up any time—or a Revolutionary Union cell member could name him while under interrogation. And he still hadn't heard what had happened to Tracy's car. Neither he nor Michael had contacted her, realizing she could be under surveillance by the FBI, but by now, if the police had picked up the car, they would surely have taken him in for questioning. They would have found his fingerprints. He remembers that when he'd been booked by the Blue Meanies they'd told him that records of a his fingerprints would be sent to the FBI. Tracy must have hidden the VW somewhere—or wrecked it. Neither she nor any of the RU people had tried to contact him. It was as if he had disappeared, had become useless, discarded. So maybe Dad's plan was working and he'd be forgotten. He'd get away with it.

Now he put on his sneakers and tied them securely. Michael would be here soon. They had planned on a walk in Tilden Park this afternoon. It was Michael's birthday and Mom was preparing a birthday dinner for him. Gina was coming, too, but she wouldn't get here until later in the afternoon. Michael had told Gina about his involvement in the RU bombing, without going into detail. He'd asked him if it was OK and he'd agreed. This afternoon would be the first time he'd spent any time with Gina since they'd broken up more than a year ago. He was relieved he didn't have to lie to her about why he'd come home. He could picture her intense green-gold eyes, and how she would look at him so directly. He had a funny feeling in his gut thinking about her, thinking of her marrying Michael. He was happy for Michael, and for her, he guessed, but it was odd. He felt that he'd really fucked up losing her. He didn't have much luck with women, did he? Gina, Tracy. He found himself grinning. How could any two women be more different!

He heard steps coming down the stairway from his parents' deck. It would be Michael, who'd been checking in with Mom and Dad. He grabbed his sweatshirt and Sierra Club canteen, which he'd already filled with tap water, and went out to meet him. Smiling, he watched Angus bounding down the stairs in front of Michael, frantically wagging his tail. "Hi, you ready?" Michael called.

"Yeah, and I see Angus expects to come." He watched as the dog raced toward Michael's car. "I haven't been up in Tilden for ages. I can do with the exercise. It seems as though I've been spending my time either in the car or hunched over a drawing board."

"Yeah, I know what you mean." Michael clapped Kim on his shoulder, and opened the car door. Before he'd climbed into the drivers seat Angus leaped inside with one smooth motion, scrambling into the back. Kim circled the car and settled next to Michael, who was watching Angus, the dog's panting muzzle poking between them from his perch on the back seat. Michael shook his head. "Dogs aren't allowed on the trails in Tilden, you know. I'm afraid, Angus, you will have to stay home."

Kim watched Angus droop. The collie knew the word stay. "Why don't we go somewhere else? Tilden gets crowded on Sundays, anyway."

"But where?"

How about that road up on the top of Grizzly Peak, just before you turn off to Tilden." He grinned. "In High School I remember taking girls up there in Dad's car to make out."

Michael laughed. "You, too? Yeah. I know the road you mean. OK. Why not?" He turned to Angus, "OK, Angus, you're on." He backed the Ford onto the street and they soon reached the top of Grizzly Peak Blvd and its sweeping view of San Francisco and the bay. Turning onto a narrow track adjacent to a grove of eucalyptus trees he parked the car and they all clambered out. Kim looped his sweatshirt around his neck and fastened the canteen on his belt. Angus had galloped down the road and was sniffing into the tall grass that bordered it. Michael locked the car and they were off.

Kim glanced at the eucalyptus trees. "I've never understood why so many of those ridiculous messy trees were planted here." "They grow fast, I guess, and all the oaks had been cut down for lumber—or fuel for the steam ships. I kind of like to watch them bend and shimmer when it's stormy."

"Yeah," Kim said giving Michael a sideways look. "They can match your mood."

Michael held Kim's look. "So how's your mood these days, brother? You've had two weeks of class. Are you. . .well, feeling less. . .stressed?"

"A little less, but it still feels stormy and dangerous out there. I keep expecting to hear the FBI on the phone when it rings or someone pounding on the door to drag me to the interrogation cellar."

"Well, maybe the Weather Underground is keeping the FBI so busy they don't have time to investigate your little shopping mall explosion. And I heard that your dear professor, Bruce Franklin, advises his followers to switch to Venceremos instead of RU, so maybe you'll get away with it, after all." He sighed. "And you're doing the right thing, going back to school, working hard."

Kim shot him a sharp look. "And in the meantime, the war goes on, guys are still getting drafted, villagers in north Vietnam are still being blown up."

Michael didn't respond. He picked up a stick and threw it for Angus to chase, who obligingly did so. Kim watched as the dog raced for the stick and brought it back to Michael, panting happily. Angus' pleasure in his task was cheering. Kim took a deep breath. He could smell the fragrance of the eucalyptus. They weren't good for much but at least they smelled good. And the sky was blue, and on his left, through a break in the trees, he spied the wide expanse of the bay, the bridges, the city, and a bulky tanker sailing slowly through the Golden Gate. He watched the ship move forward through the sun-spangled blue water. For that moment he felt his storm shift its course. Was it possible he might survive? He turned and caught up with Michael and Angus. It was good to get out, he thought, and move forward, even as slowly as the tanker sailing into the bay.

Returning from their walk an hour later, Kim unfastened his canteen and climbed into the car, first opening the back door for Angus, whose fur prickled with fox tails and bits of dried grass. Michael peered at his watch and started the car. "Gina should be at the house by now."

Kim glanced at Michael but didn't reply. His throat tightened and his breathing quickened. Within minutes he'd need to greet Gina, and he was stricken with stage fright, or something like it. He was nervous as hell. What was the protocol for greeting a former lover who was about to marry his brother? A brother who had rescued him, had stood by him, helped him recover from his depression, his scalding guilt. He gazed out the window at the passing scene, the stucco or redwood shingle houses, the glimpses of the bay, thinking of Gina. He'd loved her, but after being hit by the cop, and then dragged to jail, they didn't think the same way. He'd changed and she'd stayed the same. She'd walked out on him and he went his own way, so why was he nervous?

Now Michael drove into the driveway and they climbed the stairs to the deck and into the kitchen, Angus loping before them. Gina stood at the counter, her hands in a bowl of salad greens. Mom was by the stove. Angus let out a yelping greeting to Gina, and pranced around her gleefully. Kim watched, not moving, his feet anchored to the floor, thinking that Angus had fallen in love with her like the rest of the family had done. Gina wiped her hands on what he recognized as one of his mother's paint smocks. She stood a moment, her hands clutching the smock. "Hi, Kim," she murmured. "Did you have a good walk?" He couldn't reply, not knowing if he should touch her, kiss·her? He could feel Michael staring at the back of his head. Mom, also, had remained motionless, her eyes fixed on him. Then Gina suddenly stepped forward and kissed him on the cheek. Tentatively, he placed his hands on her shoulders, "Hi, Gina, it's good to see you. It's been a while," and he stepped back, trying to steady his voice, watching her. Her cheeks were flushed, and he noted the flicker in her eyes, a note of panic. She was nervous, too. He glanced around the room, realizing that Michael and Mom were both still staring at him—and at Gina. The room sizzled with tension. To evade their eyes, he leaned down and petted Angus. "Angus is really glad to see you, too, Gina."

Hank's voice startled him, causing him to straighten up. Dad was standing in the kitchen doorway. In an overly cheerful voice, he said, "so, here you all are. It's time to open the champagne,"

Kim tried to make sense of what Dad was saying. He glanced at Michael, whose mouth was still clamped shut. He then watched Dad as he he moved toward the refrigerator and lifted out a bottle of of Mum's, placed it on the table and reached into a high cupboards for five flutes. With a certain ceremony he popped the cap and skillfully poured the liquid into the glasses and handed them out. "OK, I know champagne is bourgeois, but it's your twenty-third birthday, Michael. And Kim and Gina, you're both over twenty-one. Lifting his glass he solemnly scanned their faces, finally focusing on Michael. "So here's to Michael. Happy birthday. Have a wonderful twenty-fourth year."

Kim lifted his glass and fastened his eyes on Michael. "Happy birthday, brother—and thanks." He shifted his gaze to Gina, who caught his look, but immediately turned to Michael. She was so beautiful, her face so perfectly oval, her green-gold eyes so expressive. He'd forgotten just how beautiful she was. Her eyes now remained on Michael. She lifted her glass and moved to his side. Kim watched as Michael slipped his arm around her waist and giving her a long, loving look, kissed her. "Thank you, Dad, Mom, Kim—and Gina. This promises to be a fantastic year for me."

Kim felt his heart clench. A dark, enveloping wave threatened to sweep over him. Michael was happy, which should please him, but instead he was envious. He'd lost so much. He'd lost Gina, but even worse, he'd lost his faith in the future. He'd lost faith in himself. And he was scared shitless. This year for him would not be fantastic. Nor any other year, maybe. For the rest of his life will he jump with fear when the telephone rings or when there's a knock at the door?

But he would work. Maybe he'd survive. And build beautiful buildings some day. Beautiful buildings for ordinary people. Somehow.

The End

Bibliography

Bentley, Eric, *Thirty Years of Treason,* Viking Press, NY, 1951.

Committee on Internal Security, House of Representatives, 92nd Congress, *Maoists: The Revolutionary Union,* The Venceremos Organization, House Report 92-1166; June 22, 1972.

Doug Engelbart Institute, *Doug's 1968 Demo: www.dougengelbart.org:*

Findley, Tim, *I was a Prisoner at Santa Rita,* San Francisco Chronicle, May 24, 1969.

Franklin, Bruce, *From the Movement Toward Revolution,* Van Nostrand Reinhold Co. NY, 1971.

Hersh, Seymour M., *The Price of Power, Kissinger in the Nixon White House,* Simon & Schuster, NY, 1983.

Montgomery, Ed, Target Date 1973, *Leftists Lift Lid on Revolutionary Plans,* S.F. Sunday Examiner & Chronicle, March 23, 1969, Page 10, section A.

Packer, George, *Blood of the Liberals,* Straus and Giroux, NY, 2000.

Rorabaugh, W. J., *Berkeley at War, the 1960's,* Oxford University Press, NY, 1989.

Rosenfeld, Seth, Subversives: *The FBI's War on Student Radicals and Reagans'Rise to Power,* Farrar, Straus and Giroux, NY, 2012.

Zaroulis, Nancy, and Sullivan, Gerald, *Who Spoke Up? American Protest Against the War in Vietnam,* 1963-1975, Doubleday & Co, Inc. NY, 1984.

About the Author

Joyce Webb Hahn, a graduate of the University of California at Berkeley, is a writer, photographer and former teacher. She has published the novels, California Yankee Under Three Flags, Viva España, Defeat, Resist and Rescue, and Heroes. Her photographs have been exhibited in Paris, Stanford, Guatemala and San Francisco. She and her husband live in Carmel Highlands, California.